Double
PLAY

A PLAYING FOR KEEPS NOVEL

Double PLAY

RANEÉ S. CLARK

To my mom, Robyn,
Who believes I'm the best writer in the world
And my dad, Doug,
Who reads romances for me. Enough said.

chapter one

SOPHIE KICKED off her turquoise stilettos and flopped onto the huge, fluffy couch that crowded the tiny living room of her apartment. Her roommate, who sat on the other side of the couch, tapping away on her laptop, didn't even look up. Sophie scooped up her shoes and held them to her chest. Despite her broken heart, at least she had these amazing shoes to adore. And they were so good to her too.

"What are you doing?" Ally asked.

So she'd finally decided to notice Sophie. "Rocket is really going to marry her," she said.

Ally tipped her head at Sophie, her eyebrows arching in a question. "What?"

"Rocket and ... that girl ... Ty. They're getting married." Sophie dropped the shoes again and buried her face in one of the pillows. When Ally didn't respond right away, Sophie lifted her head. "She's all wrong for him. He's blinded by her love of football. This is a disaster." She dropped her head again. This was as close as she'd come to crying over a guy since she and Donavan broke up.

"Wow. Who would've thought?"

Sophie tossed the pillow aside and scowled. Ally sounded mildly entertained by the news. "Is that as sympathetic as you can be?" Sophie asked. "I worked hard for two years to keep his attention, and now he's getting married. I promise, nobody saw this coming." Anthony "Rocket" Rogers was a star football player—he was going to the NFL, for heaven's sake. But it was more than just the fact that he had so much going for him or that he was charming. Rocket had cared about her. Being with him was fun. It made her happy, whether it had been on dates or just hanging out or whatever. Sure, their relationship had been on-again-off-again, but he'd always come back to her—until now. Now it was all slipping away.

"What guy chooses a girl like Ty over me?" Sophie demanded. Except Rocket had spent more and more time with that girl in the past few months and less and less time with the usual crowd. And what did he see in Ty? Sophie still didn't get it. Sure, Ty was cute, but she hid it under boxy T-shirts and too-loose jeans—not the fashionable kind either. Put that girl in a trendier outfit, maybe a purposefully oversized sweatshirt, then Sophie might get it.

Ally composed a much more consoling expression and leaned over to lay a hand on Sophie's arm. "Sorry, Soph. I know you really liked him."

Liked him? Understatement. He was her perfect match. "I had *plans*, Ally. Big. Plans." Sophie watched enough reality TV to know she'd make the perfect NFL wife. And not just by looking the part. She stood up and paced in front of the couch.

"Hands down I can do this wife-of-someone-famous thing better than Ty." Sophie wrinkled her nose and ignored the here-we-go-again sigh from Ally. "I've been networking and event planning for four years at my mom's office. I can make his dreams come true, not her. *What* is he thinking?" She spun to face Ally, throwing out her hands. Ally still had that fake sympathetic look plastered on. Sophie dropped onto the couch again. "What did I do wrong?" she asked in a smaller voice.

Ally put her arm over Sophie's shoulder and pulled Sophie toward her. "Probably nothing, sweetie."

Sophie scrutinized her outfit. A blue-and-white striped pencil skirt (to her knees, of course) and a not-too-loose white shirt with matching heels. Rocket's roommates, DJ and Sean, had tripped over themselves when they'd seen Sophie on campus earlier, but Rocket hadn't noticed her or her clothes for a while. He used to like her style—like the shorter skirts she sometimes wore off-campus. He'd admired them more than once, for sure—and then that girl had come bowling into his life and—

Sophie gulped. Her stomach turned as she remembered the night Rocket had told her he liked Ty more because she knew the real him. As he'd spoken, he'd surveyed Sophie without pleasure. Instead, he'd glowered at her the same way Donavan had when he didn't think an outfit flattered her or wasn't trendy enough. After everything she'd done to get Rocket's attention, she hadn't measured up for him either. What could Ty have done to Rocket to change how he saw Sophie?

She tapped her chin with her finger, trying to mentally work out what it was about Ty that had reeled Rocket in. When Ty had first started hanging around them when school started last September, Sophie had pegged her for just another adoring fan of Rocket's. Sure, maybe she was a novelty since she'd seemed to know everything about Rocket's career, even from back when he played in high school—and Sophie had to give Ty props for using that knowledge to steal him from her—but she'd figured that would wear off with time. It hadn't. Now Rocket was going to marry her.

"Come on, Soph, don't be too hard on yourself. It wasn't meant to be." Ally hugged her and again picked up the remote. "Let's watch some *What Not to Wear*. That'll cheer you up."

Sophie nodded, still chewing on her lip. Not meant to be? She decided what was meant to be for Sophie Pope. It wasn't like Rocket was just some guy she'd dated. She and Ally had been friends with him and his roommates for a while now. How could she let months and months of patience in her romantic pursuit of him go down the drain because of some girl who had the whole "I don't know I'm beautiful" thing going for her? Rocket would wake up one day and Ty's football knowledge wouldn't cut it anymore. Sophie couldn't let that happen to him. He needed a wife who could handle the fame that went with being a star football player. Judging by how often his girlfriend tried to tuck him away, she wasn't the right girl. Sophie was the one who knew the real Rocket Rogers. This was a guy who knew he could conquer anything he set his mind to, just like Sophie. She had to make him see that. She needed more time with, and more access to, Rocket to prove it. But how? His wedding was right around the corner, for heaven's sake.

Wedding? *That* was the answer. She hopped up off the couch and dug around in her bag for her phone. She knew just the person who could give her loads of time with Rocket, all under the guise of innocence too. Sophie had no doubt that with a couple conversations—one on one, of course—she could have Rocket back where he belonged, in her arms. Sure, this *fiancée* of his might be a nice girl, but future NFL players didn't need nice girls for wives.

Ally turned from the TV. "What're you doing?"

"Calling my mom." Sophie tapped her mom's name on her favorites' list and flicked her long, dark-brown hair out of the way as she put the phone to her ear.

"What for?" Ally squinted in confusion.

"I'm going to get her to plan Rocket's wedding. Then I'm going to get him back."

David Savage was happy for his best friend. He really was. He'd thought for sure he'd get married long before Anthony, but there ya go. While Anthony's dating binge over the last couple years—until he met Ty, of course—had been about running away from his broken heart, David had actually been looking for the right woman. And in an effort to catch up with Anthony, David had accepted every blind date Anthony and Ty had found for him. He figured Ty must know tons of girls like her.

She didn't.

So far, in the months since she and Anthony had started dating, not one of the girls they'd introduced him to measured up. Sure, Ty set a high bar, but was it that hard to find a laid-back woman who loved football as much as he did?

But David kept trying, which explained why he sat there in a booth at a pizza place near their house, listening to a woman gush over how Ty was marrying somebody like Anthony. David had dated enough girls who thought they were in love with Anthony, girls Anthony had dated a couple times and now needed another fix. David weaned them off their Rocket addictions. He didn't need that anymore. He wanted the real deal.

"So how did he ask you?" Katie leaned away from David and toward Ty, halfway over the table, her eyes shining with excitement.

Ty looked at Anthony and grinned. David turned his attention to his menu. He'd heard this story a few times in the last couple weeks. He'd also heard all the plans for this story to come about. It didn't actually surprise him that it had taken this long for Anthony to ask Ty to marry him. Commitment had been a struggle after his last girlfriend had railroaded him. But David had known Ty was the one for Anthony within days of them meeting.

"It was pretty hard to top the marching band in my front yard—" Ty said.

"Oh, yeah. I heard about that. So romantic." Katie drew out the "o" in "so" for several seconds. Then she sighed. David did have to admit Anthony's over-the-top gesture to win Ty back after he'd broken up with her was impressive. He'd gotten the BYU marching band to play in front of Ty's apartment after a football game. David had known Anthony had fallen hard for her, but grand gestures hadn't been his style—until then.

David didn't need to look up to know that Ty had that

cheesy, adoring expression on her face right now, gazing up at Anthony. "Yeah. It was," she said. "Well, Anthony went for simple this time. Um, kind of. He took me to the top of the 'Y' Trail—we'd gone there on a really great date once—and we watched Provo as the sun rose, then a ton of people dressed like runners, with numbers and everything, came running up to us, and did this flash-mob dance thing... I think he *wanted* to do simple, but he couldn't help himself." She laughed and leaned into Anthony.

"This is a once-in-a-lifetime type of thing. I had to make it good," Anthony protested. "David helped, you know."

Katie faced him for the second time during their date. (Her first and last eye contact had been when Ty introduced him.) "Really? How?"

"I walked around campus signing up people to be part of the flash-mob," David said.

"I'm still hurt you didn't let me help," a voice interrupted. He looked up to see Sophie Pope standing next to the table. "Hey, guys. Anthony. Ty. David." Her gaze drifted to each of their faces. "I'm Sophie." She stretched a long, tan arm across the table toward Katie.

Sophie wore short black shorts with her trademark high heels. Since the day he'd met Sophie a couple years ago, she'd worn heels with everything. Even when she and Ally were just coming over to watch a movie. He couldn't fault her. It made it hard not to stare at her mile-long legs.

He hurried his gaze back to Katie. Terrible date or not, checking out another girl was bad form. Unfortunately he found her looking at him for the third time, except this time with her eyes narrowed. She'd caught him staring at Sophie. Fail. Across the table, Anthony shook his head and laughed into his hand. David avoided Katie's glare and racked his brain for something to make up for it but struggled. He and Katie weren't hitting it off, and he couldn't help holding out hope for a woman whose main focus on the date was him, not the girl lucky enough to marry the star quarterback.

"I'm Katie. A friend of Ty's." Katie's voice was clipped as she shook Sophie's hand.

"Well, I don't want to interrupt for too long, but I saw you guys here, and I had to stop by and give Ty this." Sophie held a card out to Ty. "My mom's a wedding planner, and when she heard a good friend of mine"—Sophie paused and turned a dazzling smile toward Anthony. He nodded and averted his eyes to the card in Ty's hands — "had just gotten engaged, she offered to do the wedding at a steep discount." Sophie took a step closer to Anthony's side of the booth. "The quote is on the back there. Give me a call. Anthony has my number. Have a great night, guys." She wiggled her fingers at them.

"See you, Soph," David said for the table in general. Anthony, of course, had to distance himself from Sophie, since she made a play to win him back whenever they hung out lately, but David still liked her.

"Well, that was unexpected." Ty slipped the card into her purse. "So, Katie. Enough about me tonight. My mom said your softball team won a championship?"

"Yeah, our regional championship."

Softball. That explained why Ty thought he and Katie would get along. "You play ball?" he asked. He turned to give Katie his full attention. She deserved at least that after his accidental lapse of attention. It did seem unfair considering she'd spent a lot of the date fixated on the fact that Ty and Rocket were getting married, and he'd slipped up one tiny moment. Still, his mom, and Ty, expected better of him.

Katie relaxed. A little. "Yeah. For Salt Lake City Community College."

"What position?" David had already scooted closer before he realized it. Maybe he shouldn't count Katie out yet.

Her expression only slowly changed to interest. Her forgiveness wouldn't come easy. "Second base," she said.

He pointed to himself. "Center field. In high school. Football sort of took over once I started playing in college."

Katie leaned her elbow on the table and rested her head in it. "Were you good enough to play baseball in college?" She arched an eyebrow.

"Had a couple offers." He shrugged, but his grin gave away his false modesty.

"Hmmm."

He liked the way she tried not to encourage him but the corners of her lips turned up anyway. "So tell me," he asked. "If you could play any position on the field, would it still be second base? Or maybe center field?"

She gave in and let loose a fine-you're-charming smile. "I played catcher for a while in little league. I always felt pretty cool when I took the helmet off and wiped sweat out of my eyes."

"I bet you threw all the boys out on second base." David moved his arm to the top of the vinyl cushion on the back of their seat.

Katie took a sip of her drink and flashed him a smile. "At *first* base. On and off the field."

David broke into laughter and spared one glance at Ty and Anthony, who were engrossed in their own conversation, before he answered. "Of course."

Her smile widened. It felt like a small victory after the clunky start the date had gotten off to. "So what about you? If you could play any position, would you still play center field?"

"I sort of played everywhere growing up, and playing pitcher wasn't bad," he said.

"You seem like the kind of guy who'd want all the attention."

"Yeah. Ha. Ha." David tipped his chin toward Anthony. "Wonder how I ended up second fiddle to him, then."

"Bad luck?" Katie asked as Anthony and Ty joined the conversation.

"Terrible aim," Anthony said. "I mean, the kid can obviously throw since he played center field."

"Aim?" David shook his head. "Would you like to explain how I hold the record for most guys thrown out at home? That catcher's mitt is a way smaller target than anything you've thrown at."

"What would it take to convince Anthony that baseball is better than football?" Katie asked, challenge sparkling in her expression.

"If you can convince him of that, after all the years I've tried, you can have a second date with me," David said.

She tapped a finger against her lips. "Hmmm. I might need more motivation than that."

"Ouch." David chuckled. "How about you trust me and see how it goes?"

Katie pretended to study him skeptically before giving way to the laughter in her expression. "Maybe."

He was willing to bet that if he kept to his best behavior, this date might end a lot better than it had started.

"Are Sean and DJ coming?" David asked as he dumped the flag football flags into the trunk of Anthony's car.

Anthony tossed in a couple footballs before shutting the trunk and walking around to the driver's side. "Yeah. They're picking up Aaron and Ryan before they come. We should have at least ten guys. That'll make for a good game." He pulled away from the curb. "Mind if we stop at Ty's? I have to drop off the guest list I promised to give her."

"Yeah, no problem."

Anthony grinned at David as they drove. "So last night turned out well."

David snorted with laughter. "Yeah. After a pretty rocky start."

"Well, it doesn't look like you'll need to worry about getting a date for the wedding. She was into you."

David pushed open his door as they pulled up to Ty's a few blocks away. "Only after she found out I played baseball."

"You going to ask her out again?" Anthony asked as they hurried up the steps.

"Yeah. Probably. She seemed pretty cool, once she got over her awe of Ty marrying you and started acting normal again. I don't get it. It used to be girls falling all over you—now they're falling all over Ty because of you. I've known you awhile. You're not that great."

Ty swung open the door and hugged Anthony. "Says you. And you're in the minority. Didn't he get something like a ninety for his grade on the draft?"

"Ninety-four-point-seven. The highest." Anthony held out a hand for David to fist bump.

"And according to what I read on the website, that means we're talking about a future Hall-of-Famer. A top pick." She patted Anthony on the chest.

"Okay, okay." David held up his hands in surrender.

"Your grade was very good too, Beast. Seventy-two? You'll go in the second or third round."

"Who showed her that website?" David shook his head and walked past her into the apartment, spotting Ty's roommate standing by the kitchen table, which was littered with papers and a couple notebooks.

"Ty, what's this?" Rosie held out the card Sophie had given Ty the night before.

"One of Anthony's old girlfriends offered up her mom's wedding planning services."

"And the number on the back here? Is that the down payment?" Rosie asked.

"Down payment? No." Ty eyed Rosie. "I hope not. Sophie said that was the price she would give us."

Rosie's mouth dropped. "June Pope offered to plan your wedding for that?"

"Wait a second." Ty held a hand up. "How do you even know about her and if this is a good price? It's expensive." Ty had a point. Rosie acted like Sophie's mom was some kind of celebrity.

Rosie blushed and rolled her gaze to the ceiling. "I'm a planner, guys, so yeah, I've looked into wedding planning and the rates and all that stuff—I plan. I just do." She glared at Ty, daring her to challenge this explanation or make fun of it.

"You have your wedding planned and you don't even—" David started, but a swift elbow to his gut from Anthony cut him off.

"Yes." Ty raised an eyebrow at him. "Girls plan their weddings long before there's a reason to. Now clearly, Rosie has taken this to another level, but it's Rosie, guys. Nobody's surprised."

"Wow. Thanks for that glowing defense." Rosie folded her arms and shook her head at Ty. Then Rosie took a deep breath and Ty tried not to laugh.

"Don't worry," Ty said. "Rosie's taking a moment to figure out how to boss me around without sounding like she is."

Rosie finally smiled but waved the card around in an excited way. "June Pope planned Valerie Keen's wedding—you know, that LDS girl who won *Bachelor* last year?"

Ty nodded, impressed but not won over. "So she's good?"

"She's the *best*. She can hook you up with awesome stuff in the area. And that price? It's a steal."

"But won't all the connections she has cost more, even if she can get them for us?" Ty tapped the card against her hand and frowned.

"I don't know. But it's worth making an appointment to talk to her," Rosie said.

Ty turned to Anthony, her lips pressed into a line and head tilted in skepticism. "What do you think?"

David ducked his head. If he knew Sophie like he thought he

Ranee S. Clark

did, she'd made the offer irresistible for a reason. What did she get from her mom planning Anthony's wedding? Even though Ty and Anthony had been dating for over six months, Sophie had accosted him every time they were in the same room, whether Ty was there or not. This was another ploy to get Anthony's attention back. It wasn't the first time David had witnessed Sophie blow over everyone in her path to get something she wanted. Like the time she wanted to plan Anthony's birthday party and had refused to listen when David and his other roommates protested that they were having a *Madden NFL* tournament complete with pizza and soda. Instead of giving up, she'd outdone them. She'd rented a huge screen to play the video game on and brought excellent food—pizza *and* buffalo wings, sandwiches, and every other game-night appetizer you could think of.

"It's up to you, Ty. If she's good, maybe you should consider it," Anthony said.

She nodded slowly. She was smart. David wondered if the same possibilities that had run through his head had occurred to her as well. She replaced her contemplative look with a smile and pushed Anthony toward the door. "Go do your boy things. David's getting itchy over there."

Anthony pulled Ty toward him to kiss her goodbye. David took that as his cue to head out. He opened the door and stepped out onto the landing, waiting in silence for Anthony to finish his goodbye. He was happy for Anthony, but now that the guy David never thought would settle down was settling down before him, it did make David itchy. Itchy for a woman who could put him under her thumb the way Ty had Anthony. He didn't need a woman to follow his every career step and read every article and watch every game the way Ty had for Anthony before they met. But he certainly wouldn't mind one as loyal as she was. Someone who could trust him with her heart the way Ty had given hers to Anthony, no matter where it led.

He made a decision. He pulled out his phone to text Katie.

DAVID

If I can get tickets to a Bees game, can I talk you into going with me?

KATIE

Maybe you should leave the tickets to me. I know someone who could get us pretty good seats. Saturday night?

David chuckled to himself.

DAVID

I'm going to pretend I'm not wondering if that someone is on the team. But since more than likely he's not as handsome as me, I'll let it slide. Saturday's great. Where should I pick you up?

KATIE

Just to ease your mind, I'll let you in on a secret. It's the manager's daughter. We played softball together in high school.

Anthony emerged, trying to wipe away his goofy grin with his hand.

"Oh, come up for air?" David double-checked the address Katie had texted him, then shoved the phone into his pocket.

"Mature." Anthony slugged him in the arm. They headed down the steps together. "Are you as suspicious of Sophie's offer as I am?" he asked.

"Yup. I don't have to tell you what she's up to."

"One final try at breaking up me and Ty. Not that it'd be successful, but I've seen enough movies to know that she could get me into a sticky situation if I let her." He sighed and shook his head. "And the last thing I want is for something to ruin the wedding for Ty."

"Then tell Ty that. I get the feeling she wouldn't mind turning this offer down. She's never struck me as the type of girl who hires a wedding planner. Aren't you guys doing your reception in the stadium or something?"

Anthony chuckled. "Nice. No, but that's exactly why Ty should get this wedding planner—should get the best wedding planner. It's her big day, and I want her to have everything she could possibly desire."

"Well, I guess you're going to have to be extra careful." David shrugged.

"Yeah. I guess."

An inkling of pity ran through David. But just an inkling. What did Anthony have to whine about when he was marrying someone like Ty?

chapter two

THE THRUM of music pulsating from inside the parking garage proved David was late. Music for the rooftop concert series didn't start until seven thirty, and he was supposed to meet the group coming to hear one of his teammates, Ryan, and his band play at six thirty. Hopefully they'd saved a spot for him. David had started studying for a final after he got home from lifting weights that afternoon and had almost forgotten his plans.

People, blankets, and camp chairs packed the rooftop, as they usually did during the concerts, so David scanned the heads of the concert-goers as he texted Sean. Not that finding his six-eight, 250-pound roommate was ever hard. David spotted him closer to the back of the crowd, the spaces around him filled with his football teammates and most of his regular crowd. Sophie Pope and her roommate Ally sat next to DJ and another running back, Aaron. David chuckled to himself. As Anthony's closest friends, if he showed up, he'd sit by them. And Sophie knew that. He strode right over and dropped into the tiny space between her and Ally.

"Ladies, do you mind if I take this seat?" he asked.

Ally laughed, scooting over to give him space. "No problem." Sophie glanced past him, her lips drawing down in disappointment.

"No Anthony tonight. Sorry," David said, smirking at her.

"Who said I was looking for Anthony?" She met his gaze with an indifferent expression.

"Aren't you always looking for Anthony?" he teased. Since her plan to win him back was so obvious, David wanted to challenge her. "Not sure if you've heard yet or not, but he's getting married."

Sophie's eyes narrowed. "What he's doing is making a big mistake, but Anthony's smart. He'll figure that out before it's too late."

David laughed and turned toward the band playing—not Ryan's yet. Sophie had never understood what made Ty so attractive. Probably because Ty didn't care about fashion or consider flirting a skill like Sophie did. And nothing David said about the qualities that made Anthony love Ty would convince Sophie, so he didn't bother. He did study her for a moment when she looked away, wondering if losing Anthony had really broken her heart of if he was just another goal she needed to achieve. Sophie had always been driven. Sometimes the other girls that hung out with their crowd stopped coming around more because of her intense personality than because they'd dated Anthony and/or David and then moved on.

"You guys ready for finals?" he asked, changing the subject.

Ally groaned and shook her head, but Sophie kept on bobbing to the beat and stared toward the stage. "I'm going to rock mine, of course," she said.

"Have a secret strategy you want to share?" David nudged her with his elbow.

She swept her long brown hair off her back and over her shoulder with one hand before answering. "Studying. It might help if you did that instead of play football and video games all the time." If any other woman had overlooked how hard David worked to get good grades in school too, it might have bothered him. But he and Sophie had studied together enough that he knew when she was teasing him, even if she could keep a straight face while she said it.

"Hmmm. I'll have to try it out. Sounds boring though." He looked over his shoulder at Sean and the others behind him. "Anybody bring anything to eat? I'm starving."

"I would have thought eating is what made you late." Ally handed him a bag of pretzels.

"Actually I was too busy playing video games to notice the time," he said, taking the bag gratefully. "Or studying. I can't remember."

"Where's Dreamy?" Sean asked, referring to Anthony. His fans all knew the nickname Rocket, but Anthony had a million more— Dreamy was how his roommates usually referred to him, thanks to his dating past. Sean reached over David into the bag and took half of its contents away in one of his massive hands.

"Him and Ty said something about getting slushies"—David made dramatic mock quotes in the air with his fingers—"or some kind of nonsense like that. He said not to tell Ryan if he didn't show up."

"They're just glad to finally be rid of you," DJ said, and the others laughed.

"Hey." David pretended to be offended. "Anthony was mine first."

"If that's true, how come you're not more sympathetic to me?" Sophie asked.

He leaned closer to her. "Maybe I'm the one who truly loves him and wants him to be happy."

"And there's my point, Beast. Ty can't actually make him happy in the end, and I can. You'll see." Sophie held his gaze, her eyebrows raised, daring him to contradict her. He'd once watched Sophie convince a girl that Rocket would break her heart and not to risk the date the girl had fought so hard to get. And following that outstanding performance, Sophie had told Anthony she would be going out with him instead. No doubt she had a stinking good argument for not giving up. He wasn't about to go into that with her.

But he had better warn Anthony that Sophie meant business.

Much to David's chagrin, his second date with Katie was not off to a great start. Katie's friend from high school who'd gotten them the seats—right behind home plate, two rows up —had stopped by to see what they thought of their seats. (Awesome, of course, which both David and Katie reiterated a couple times.) And now the friend, Abbey, was flirting with David, and he was trying not to flirt but to still be nice since she had gotten them awesome seats. Katie did *not* appreciate the difference—or she plain didn't appreciate his nice-flirting. Either way, he wondered if escaping to get them food would be acceptable.

Ah, heck. If he didn't get out of there soon, the possibility of this date continuing was slim. He hopped out of his seat. "I'm going to get us something to eat. What do you prefer? Hot dog? Pizza? Nachos? You name it. My treat." He flashed his best, I-apologize-for-being-handsome smile.

Katie rolled her eyes. Maybe she didn't understand the smile either. "Pizza sounds good. Thanks."

As David hurried up the stairs toward the concession concourse, his thoughts jumped to Sophie. She'd never get all out of joint because someone flirted with her date. Considering the confident way she'd acted at the concert about winning Anthony back, she'd probably step up and take control. She hadn't even flinched when David had challenged her. Maybe she wasn't into sports, but he could still appreciate the competitor in her.

When he came back with the pizza, Abbey had left. It gave David some hope that he might salvage the rest of the date. He handed Katie her plate and the soda he'd gotten her before sitting down.

After taking her first sip, she made a face that she tried to cover. "Um, what'd you get me?"

"Root beer. It was either that or the syrupy stuff they call lemon-lime soda. Or Pepsi, I guess. I wasn't sure about your stance on caffeine..." He grinned. Truth be told, he'd never met anyone, woman or otherwise, who didn't like root beer. He'd assumed it was a safe bet. Judging by the way she wrinkled her nose, he'd assumed wrong.

"What'd you get?" she asked.

"Root beer." He arched an eyebrow. "Want me to go get you something else?"

"Not to be a pain, but ... would you?" She handed him her cup.

He'd expected an answer like, "No, don't worry about it," so this caught him by surprise. Asking him to go get her a different soda seemed more like something Sophie would pull, not down-to-earth Katie.

Or he'd thought she was down to earth.

Red pooled in her cheeks, presumably at his hesitance, and she pulled back the cup, which she'd been holding between them. Her shoulders stiffened. "Uh, sorry. You offered. I thought you meant it."

David wiped the surprised expression from his face and grabbed her soda. "I did. They're, uh, not going to take this back, so I'll save it for later. And what do you want?"

"Pepsi, please." She ventured an embarrassed smile as he stood. "Diet, if they have it."

"You got it." He put the root beer in the cup holder between them. "I'll be right back." He scooted past the other people taking their seats and bounded up the steps to the concession stand.

He returned ten minutes later with a new soda and a cup of ice cream that had cost him an arm and a leg. "Your soda." He handed it over with an exaggerated bow and won a laugh from her. "And I got 'I'm-sorry-this-date-started-out-so-bad' chocolate ice cream." He held it toward her as he pushed down the seat of his chair and sat down.

"Ahhh, um, thanks. This is good for now, though. You'd better eat it." She took a bite of her pizza and then picked at the crust.

"You don't like chocolate ice cream?" he guessed. "Or ice cream at all?"

She shrugged. "Just chocolate ice cream."

David tried to process that. He'd wanted to do something to make up for the situation with Abbey and getting the drink wrong. In retrospect, maybe he'd made things worse by trying to guess again, but didn't all girls love everything chocolate? It was one of the first things his mom had taught him when he turned sixteen: when in doubt, buy a woman chocolate. Maybe he should have gone with a candy bar. But there'd been so many choices, and really, who said no to ice cream?

He forced a laugh. "Well, more for me then." He dug his spoon into it and took out a huge bite. "Again, I should have asked. Guess I'm bad at that." Concentrating on the field, he shoved the bite into his mouth. He winced at the ice cream headache he got a few seconds later.

"It's okay." Katie patted his leg. "It's the thought that counts."

He moved to take her hand. This was her first effort at physical contact between them. "Thanks."

Then she pulled her hand away and focused on the field.

When did dating get this hard?

Neither one said much as they ate their food and watched the game. Since he finished his hot dog long before Katie finished her pizza, he leaned forward and got into the action on the field. The sky shone a gorgeous, clear, bright blue. Perfect day for baseball. Watching the guys down on the field brought back his own memories from playing center field. Sweaty hair underneath his hat, warmth at his back, almost losing fly balls in the sun. Good, good days.

So far the game was pretty close, with neither team scoring in the first two innings. When one of the Bees players rounded third base and headed for home at the same time the opposing team's center-fielder threw the ball, David whooped and cheered the runner on, then slumped into his seat in good-natured disappointment when the ball made it to home plate first and the catcher tagged the runner out.

"You'd think it was pretty girls down there playing, considering how into this game you are." Katie didn't look at him as she made the comment, and though he tried, David couldn't pick a joke out of it. Still smarting from Abbey's flirting?

"Uh." David attempted a light-hearted chuckle as he tried to come up with a response. "Been a while since I went to a game in person. My friends are football fans, you know." He nodded toward the field, getting caught up for a minute as the batter fouled off what would have been a great line-drive if it'd landed a couple more inches to the left.

"Guess I'm one of those people who'd rather play than watch. I thought it might be a good place for us to get to know each other, though." Katie forced a smile. "But I'll admit, it's better than watching a football game." She elbowed him playfully.

David sounded stupid when he laughed, since he loved football as much as he did baseball, but Katie had meant it as a joke —she must have. Nobody dissed their date's whole profession outright like that. And okay, so he should pay more attention to her than the game. This was a date. But Ty and Anthony watched sports together all the time, and their interactions didn't take this much effort. In fact, more often than not, when David watched with them, he found himself insanely jealous of the way they could dissect a play together or hold an in-depth discussion about the action on the field. Right after they met, Anthony had come home raving about how she'd analyzed an upcoming game with him in class. So just because she wasn't playing, Katie couldn't get into the game?

"We'll have to agree to disagree on football. But I would

always rather play than watch, so we can find some common ground there." He tapped his fingers against his thigh, hoping she'd come up with something for them to talk about. For the life of him, he could only think about sports at the moment. Maybe he should steer the conversation back toward her softball career. That's how he'd saved the day during their last date. They'd talked easily once they'd discovered their shared love of baseball, but of course he'd also had Ty and Anthony to help. Katie took a sip of her soda, half-watching the game and half-watching the people around them.

"So what made you choose football over baseball?" she asked after several moments of awkward silence.

"To be honest, Anthony talked me into it. We played amazing together in high school, and when Coach asked Anthony to come on, Anthony asked for a spot for me too. I'm glad I did." Even though this was kind of the getting-to-know you conversation the date needed, awkwardness still tinged it, especially since, at his answer, she let a short breath escape that almost sounded like a laugh. He kept his expression impassive at her continued condescension of football. He was probably getting defensive and reading into her reactions.

"Oh—" she started and then the batter hit a nice line drive past the right fielder and got to second base on it. David whooped and Katie finished with a scowl, "—really." She leaned away from him.

"Uh, sorry?" he offered, not picking up on what he'd done to tick her off now. He'd been listening. It was one cheer. "Nice hit," he tried. Katie challenged his charms more than he cared to admit.

"Not bad. I'd like to see one of these guys hit a fast-pitch softball."

David clamped his mouth shut so he wouldn't argue and make this situation worse. They would have to agree to disagree on this issue. He had his opinions on pro-baseball players being able to hit softballs, but he didn't want to diminish the incredible talents of softball players either.

"It'd be tough getting used to," he said to pacify her. She nodded and stared at the field. "So you like playing for Salt Lake?" he asked. This topic might be a good way to get to know her.

"Why wouldn't I?" she challenged him. "Since it's not as big as BYU, they must not be as good, right?"

David rested his elbow on the armrest, away from Katie. "Nope. Didn't think that. Just making conversation."

"Sure."

David didn't know if that was in answer to his question or a sarcastic retort about his motives. Sheesh. This date was tanking hard. So strike talking about baseball, maybe he could figure out something else about her.

"If you're not a chocolate ice cream girl, what's your go-to flavor?" He purposefully ignored the runner dancing around second base, getting ready to steal.

"I don't eat a lot of ice cream." She poked at David's ribs and even managed a teasing expression. "I know you football players can eat whatever you want, then lift some weights, but I've got to keep the extra pounds off to stay quick."

She was happy—a little bit—so David didn't argue about how fast he had to run to beat defensive players down the field or how he didn't exactly sit around eating ice cream all day and maintain abs like his.

She clapped. "Now, I'll admit that was a great steal. Did you see that?" She pointed at the field.

No. He hadn't. He didn't bother now either. "Mint chocolate chip is my favorite. Ice cream," he added when she frowned in confusion. "It's basically all we have in our freezer. I eat it all the time then do a couple arm curls before bed and call it good. That's how I got the awesomely toned and sculpted body before you." He let all the sarcasm he meant in that statement drip off it.

She didn't pick up on it. She laughed. "I knew it. It's so unfair that boys can do that. I swear, I'll have a skimpy salad for lunch and still gain a couple pounds."

"Yeah, sucks to be me." David faked another smile. He took a deep breath to prepare for the sacrifice the next conversation topic would make. "So, it's pretty cool how Anthony proposed to Ty, right?"

Katie's eyes lit up. "Definitely. How many runners were you able to get?"

"Over a hundred," he said, settling back in his seat and preparing not to watch any of the game and talk way more about Anthony and Ty than he ever wanted to.

Talking about wedding stuff and then finding something else to talk about when they exhausted that subject sucked the life out of David for the next hour and a half. He almost booed when the Bees tied the game at two to two in the bottom of the ninth and sent the game into extra innings.

But it was almost over. Abbey had offered to introduce them to some of the guys on the team, and then he could take Katie home.

Then David heard, "Savage? Is that you, Beast?"

He grinned at the familiar voice. Seeing his old teammate, Dallas Cooke, might make up for the difficult couple of hours he'd spent in Katie's company. To say the two of them hadn't clicked would be an understatement.

Dallas hurried toward them, tucking his mitt under his arm as he slung his hand forward to shake David's. He pulled David into a half-hug and pounded him on the back. "It's been forever."

"What's up, Cooke?" David asked.

"Keep hoping for a call-up, you know?" Dallas nodded toward Katie. "Who's your lovely friend? Just friend, right? I hope?" He held out his hand to shake hers.

She answered before he could, with full-fledged delight. More than David had gotten. "Yeah. Friends. I'm Katie." She let her hand linger in his.

David officially gave the date up as a failure. Of epic proportions. He swallowed back a retort and laughed—again. By now his automatic, but forced, response to keep things light between them wore thin. But the reminder that he still stood there pulled her hand from Dallas's, and she tittered nervously.

"So, Beast?" she asked, glancing between the two of them. "How'd you get that nickname?"

"Savage Beast, you know?" Cooke explained. "Anthony Rogers started it in high school."

"Cool." Katie beamed at Cooke instead of David.

"Let's go meet some of the other guys while Dallas and David talk." Abbey grimaced at David, then took Katie's arm and hauled her off.

"Good to meet you." Dallas waved as they walked away.

David ignored Katie's energetic wave back. "But seriously, Katie knows Abbey, so feel free to ask for her number when we leave," he said to Dallas when the girls walked out of earshot.

"You're already counting her out?"

"Let's just say this date hasn't been the best."

"I've heard you've had more than a few ladies to choose from. Guess they can't all measure up." Dallas shrugged and cast another look over his shoulder. "Your loss."

"Listen—" David was on the verge of defending his choice, but he sighed. No use in talking badly about Katie, even if she didn't like chocolate ice cream. Dallas could discover it all on his own. "Some days I'm ready to move on. Different girls."

"What? 'Cause you've dated all the ones here already?"

"I think so." David punched Dallas in the arm. "Gonna play NFL?"

"Sure. If I get drafted."

Dallas squinted at David then patted his shoulder. "Lucky. Hey, I'd hate to keep you from enjoying the rest of your date. We should catch up some time." He waved his mitt and took off, winking at Katie on his way by.

Shoving his hands in his pockets, David was left to ponder the way Dallas's jaw stiffened and the slight frown he'd given David after he asked about going into the NFL. Was he jealous? David pushed it aside and went to catch up with Abbey and Katie. He wondered how mad it would make Katie if he asked Abbey out. Later, of course. Not today.

After such an exhausting date, David wanted nothing more than to chill in front of their sixty-inch screen with a video game controller in his hands. But when he got home, DJ, Aaron, and a couple girls from a few houses down already had it staked out.

"I'm in the next round," he said as he passed the couch.

"Sure," DJ said, and Aaron reached up to bump David's fist as he went by. They were playing some racing game, and despite Aaron's inattention and DJ playing with only his left hand, they were both embarrassing the two girls, who couldn't keep their cars on the road. They really put their muscles into it by leaning into DJ at every turn possible. DJ wrapped his free arm around them if he could, cheering them on and urging them closer to him. David's other roommate, Sean, stood behind the couch, watching the game.

David paused before heading into the kitchen, resting against the archway that separated their cluttered living room from the tiny kitchen. "You guys seen Anthony?"

"Nah." Aaron glanced back at David to answer and still didn't crash his car around one of the tight corners.

"Yeah, right," DJ said. Sean gave David a knowing look. Anthony had gotten pretty scarce when he'd started dating Ty, and it had only gotten worse now that they were engaged. If David hadn't seen him sleeping in his bed from time to time, he'd wonder if Anthony had already moved out. When Sophie had teased David about him not wanting to give Anthony up either, she'd struck close to home. Maybe that's why he'd upped the ante for getting married and accepted every blind date Ty could think of. He and Anthony had been inseparable since middle school. They'd lived next door to each other, though lived *with* each other would've been a more accurate statement. Most nights David stayed at Anthony's or Anthony stayed at David's. Once Anthony got married, it would be the first time besides their missions that they'd really be separated. Even when David had been in Indiana and Anthony had been in Guatemala while on their missions, there'd always been a plan for them to live together once they got back. The desire to have what Anthony had found with Ty—more than just a girlfriend or a fiancée, but another best friend—burned strong in David. The disappointment that things hadn't gone anywhere with Katie hurt all the more for it.

David headed for the ancient fridge in the kitchen as a tap at the front door announced the entrance of Ally and Sophie.

"We have cake," Ally said in a sing-song voice, holding up a box as she marched toward the kitchen. Sean abandoned the uninteresting game to follow them. As the center of the football team, the beefy lineman filled up any room.

"Who do we have to thank for this?" he asked, taking the box from Ally to set on the counter. David forgot about whatever he was searching for in the fridge and reached for a stack of paper plates on top to hand to his roommate.

"The Jensen-Kole reception," Sophie said, scanning the room. She frowned when she didn't find Anthony, but it didn't seem to surprise her.

"Tell me you're going to keep working for your mom after graduation, Sophie," Sean said, lifting a few pieces onto his plate before backing away. "You always bring the good food. Who knows what we'll have to choke down if you leave us to Ally."

"Hey." Ally swatted Sean and shook her head. Since David stood within reach of Sean, and because he didn't feel like making his way across the kitchen for cake, David stole a piece of Sean's.

"*You're* sticking around?" Sophie questioned Sean, hopping

onto an empty space on the counter and kicking off a pair of silver heels. She must have come straight from working the reception, since she still wore a fancy-looking green dress. "I thought you'd be on the next plane out of here after the draft."

"I'm not going to the NFL," Sean said around half of one of his pieces. "I've got a couple teaching and assistant coaching offers at some high schools nearby." He shoved more cake in his mouth. Sean avoided talking with most people about his decision to teach instead of pursue his own career in football, and filling his mouth gave him an excuse not to talk for a few minutes. Even though Sean looked forward to working with kids both on and off the field, it surprised most people that he didn't have his eye on playing football professionally. And he didn't like defending his choice over it.

Sophie nodded at him before she reached over and wiped a finger across the top of one of his pieces and licked the frosting off. "You'll make a good coach," she said.

Sean colored at her compliment, and David's shoulders shook from silent laughter at the way he struggled to swallow. "Well, are you going to hang around?" Sean asked Sophie when he got it down.

Sophie shrugged. "I do have a pretty good job already with some awesome perks. We'll see what else comes up."

Ally peered around the archway that separated the kitchen and living room and then lowered her voice to a whisper. "You guys know Shayli really likes DJ, right? Maybe you could help that along."

Both David and Sean studied the people on the couch. The woman Ally meant was leaning into DJ again. "How are we supposed to do that?" David asked. "It looks like she's doing pretty good on her own."

Ally sighed. "Tell him, of course. DJ is a big flirt. Shayli doesn't think he likes her any more than he likes all the other girls that come through here."

David and Sean both held back laughs at Ally's annoyance,

and even Sophie showed amusement. Ally swatted Sean again. "All the girls?" Sean repeated.

"It's like they think we have a harem hiding out somewhere." David crossed the kitchen to snag another piece of cake. Instead of going back to his original place, he leaned against the counter next to Sophie. "Does that mean you two are part of it?"

"You wish," Sophie said.

"You're around enough. Wouldn't that make you the head concubine or something?" David asked teasingly and leaned into Sophie.

"He has a point," Sean said. "You guys are here more than Anthony lately."

"Maybe we can work out a code or something. Leave a tie on the door if he's around. Black if he's here without Ty." David laughed as Sophie glared at him.

"*I* don't need your help with guys. Ever. I know how to handle Anthony." Sophie folded her arms.

She had a really attractive pouting expression. She didn't do the cliché, bottom-lip-out thing, but some vulnerability showed in her eyes, and she just had great lips in general. How come, after a couple years of being friends, he hadn't dated Sophie? She wasn't really his type, but neither were a lot of the others girls he'd dated who'd gone out with Anthony first, back before Ty. Maybe because Sophie hadn't given up on Anthony like the other girls so he'd never really considered her available.

"Anthony's pretty much never without Ty," Sean said, patting Sophie on the shoulder as he passed to go back to the living room.

David might have been the only one who heard Sophie mutter, "Tell me about it."

And he absolutely agreed with her.

chapter three

"OOOOOH. What are you so spiffed up for?" Ally leaned against the doorway of Sophie's room Monday morning and whistled.

"Ty Daws called Mom. She and Anthony are meeting with her today." Sophie held up another shirt, this time a simple, white button-up. Tucked in to the high-waisted, short, black pencil skirt she already wore? And maybe a belt.

"She went for it?" Ally walked into the room and took the shirt with a shake of her head.

"Yeah ... what are you doing?"

"Anthony's engaged now. A short skirt's going to make him avert his eyes, especially in front of Ty. Who doesn't, by the way, seem like the type of girl to hire a wedding planner."

"It surprised me too. Long shot, I guess you could say, but now that I've got it... Well, what do you propose I do to get him back?" She frowned at the pair of black stilettos with a flower on the heel that she already wore. She'd bought them just for today, and they would have gone perfectly with the outfit she'd chosen.

Ally plunged into Sophie's closet and came out with a cap-sleeved, black sheath dress and a wide, turquoise belt. "This." She tossed the dress at Sophie. "It hits *almost* to your knees, but with this belt, it's going to show off your knock-out figure."

Sophie scowled. She saved dresses like that for church, not for reeling in guys. But Ally had a point. "Okay, I'll try your way this time."

"You'll thank me. Good luck." Ally bit her bottom lip and then walked out with a half-wave.

What was that look for? Sophie shrugged it off and watched Ally's jean-clad figure disappear down the hallway. Ally dressed cute, but the loose, wide-leg jeans made her appear boxy—hard to do with a skinny-broomstick figure like Ally's. A pair of flair jeans would really work better.

Sophie stopped herself. Her roommate had made Sophie promise long ago to quit making outfit suggestions, a habit of Sophie's that not everyone appreciated. She couldn't help the knack she had for how to flatter others' figures.

A glance at the clock told Sophie she didn't have time for ruminating. She needed to get dressed and down to her mom's office.

When Sophie arrived at the office suite at Jamestown Square, she hurried past the reception area with little more than a wave for Kaylie, the receptionist, and Jessica, her mom's assistant, who sat next to Kaylie at the front desk. When Sophie reached her mom's office, June paced near the window, talking on the phone, so Sophie plopped her purse on the desk and settled into June's chair.

June ended the call a few seconds later. Good thing Sophie had opted not to wear the pencil skirt. Her mother wore a longer version with a bright yellow blouse, tucked in, like Sophie had planned. Of course her great taste came from her mom.

"Hello, Soph." June crossed the room in quick strides and leaned against the desk.

"Hey, Mom."

June folded her arms. "Now, tell me why I'm doing this for pocket change."

"You're doing it for Rocket Rogers, Mom. He's a popular guy, and this is going to be great for you."

"If you haven't noticed, I'm doing pretty well for myself these days." June tapped one of her long fingers against her elbow.

"Anthony is a very good friend of mine." Sophie ignored that both of June's eyebrows shot up. Sophie may never have hidden her attraction to him, but she hadn't ever elaborated either. After a week or two of dating, he would usually start dating someone else, and it would take more planning and effort from Sophie to get him back again. Their relationship had just never quite reached the meet-the-parents stage.

"He's a good friend," Sophie repeated, "and I want you to help him out. For me."

June shook her head. "And is this also the explanation for the bigger responsibilities you want me to give you? So you can help your good friend?"

Sophie twisted back and forth in the chair, avoiding June's gaze. "Sure. I thought since I talked your price down so far, you'd appreciate my free labor."

June chuckled. "You make it sound like I'm sending you down a coal mine. Fabulous shoes."

Again, Sophie couldn't help kicking up her feet to admire the shoes. "Thanks."

"Before Miss Daws gets here, I need your opinion." June bent over and flicked her mouse, her wide computer screen lighting up. "What do you think of this dress?"

Sophie leaned forward to study it. Shimmery lavender with a draped neckline and ruching through the waist and skirt. "Depends on the figure of whoever wants it." She pushed away from the computer. "Mother-of-the-bride dress?"

June put a hand on her hip, a move Sophie had imitated since she was little. "Not unless you have something to tell me. I need a dress that's not too outspoken for the Carr wedding, but it has to stand up to all the great dresses that will already be there."

"You'd rock it, and you know it. You didn't really need my opinion." But Sophie still liked that June had humored her.

"I *did* need it. You can never be sure with ruching. Sometimes the gathering bunches in all the wrong places. Come with me to try it on later?"

"I have class after this meeting, but we could take a long lunch?" Sophie suggested.

"Done."

June's assistant, Jessica, tapped on the already open door. "Ms. Pope? Ty Daws is here."

"Send her right in." Sophie resisted the urge to rub her hands together in anticipation.

Jessica quirked her lips before questioning June with a raise of her eyebrows. "Yes, send them in." June laughed. She patted Sophie's shoulder as Jessica disappeared back down the hallway. "You'd better give me that chair, don't you think?"

"Well, if you insist." Sophie would appear at a better advantage standing anyway. She traded places with her mother at the massive oak desk and crossed her ankles. Ty walked through first. She'd dressed up for the appointment—well, for Ty anyway —in a jersey tee with ruffled sleeves. But she still wore jeans. Not even a trendy, fashionable pair. Sophie had stopped counting the number of times she'd bit her tongue to keep from suggesting that Ty try on a pair of straight jeans or a tailored wide leg. They'd look so great on her petite figure.

She was not here to help Ty look better. But she turned on her anything-for-the-bride manners anyway. "Hi, Ty." She fluttered her fingers and peered past her for Anthony. She caught sight of a middle-aged woman instead.

"Hey Sophie, this is my mom, Kim," Ty said. "Since she's paying, it made more sense for her to come and see what you guys can do for me." In one glance Sophie could tell Ty didn't get her fashion sense from her mom. Though Sophie would call it boring, Kim Daws at least knew how to flatter her figure to its best. She created curves on her thin, athletic figure—so much like her daughter's—by wearing a white button-down shirt with a feminine cut tucked into a pair of dark-wash, boot-cut jeans, and topped it off with a simple, gold bar necklace.

"Of course," June said, coming forward to shake both their hands. "Would you like to take a seat?" She gestured to two of the armchairs across from the desk. As the women sat, Sophie clamped down her disappointment. Anthony might try to beg out of as many wedding-planning responsibilities as he could; lots of grooms did. She should have seen that coming. Somehow she'd have to make him part of this.

"We'll want to make sure we include both you and Anthony in the planning process in order to make the wedding a success," Sophie said.

"Of course." Ty met her gaze and nodded in a knowing way that made Sophie wish she'd kept quiet. Ty leaned forward. "So, Ms. Pope. I hope you don't mind me asking, but there's something I need to get out of the way right off," she said. "This price is amazing—thank you, by the way—but since I'm not familiar with wedding planning, I'm not sure exactly what services it includes."

"Excellent question, dear," June said, her expression relaxed and pleasant to put Ty at ease. June made people comfortable, a fitting gift for someone who dealt with brides on a constant basis. "That price is for my services in planning the event— helping you find venues and scheduling them, finding the people you'll need, like photographers, someone to make the cake—you get the picture. Now..." She took a breath and shared a quick look with Sophie. "If your dates are flexible, I can arrange a package deal for not much more that would include a fantastic venue for the reception, a top-notch photographer, the best caterer in town, an amazing cake, and breathtaking decorations. We can even pull some strings to get you a dress."

Ty scanned the room, probably taking in June's flawless, elegant taste. She sat back in her chair, staring first at Sophie then back to June. "Really?"

"Yes. Really. Shall we look at some pictures to help you decide?"

"Yeah, good idea." Ty glanced at her mom, who gave her an

encouraging nod. Sophie could see in both their faces that June had them on the hook.

"Sophie? Why don't you get me the outdoors venue binder, please?" June asked.

Sophie stood with a proud grin at the excitement that jumped to Ty's face. Yes, outdoor would be perfect for Ty and Anthony. If it happened. Which it wouldn't. Sophie retrieved the binder and set it down on the desk in front of Ty.

"Scoot on up, dear," June invited.

The first breathy "Oh" sigh that left Ty's lips clinched it. Forty-five minutes later, June and Sophie left Ty and her mom for a few minutes of private discussion. Ty signed the contract that afternoon.

"Remember the time I talked Coach Hill into playing Cal so you could get a date with his sister?" Anthony asked David when he set his tray down next to his at the Cougareat Tuesday afternoon.

"Yeah…" David studied Anthony, wondering why he'd bring up something that happened in high school out of the blue like that. He scooted out his chair and sat without taking his eyes off his best friend.

"And the time I picked Kurt Collins for my football team so you could have McKayla Parker on your team?"

David laughed. "Dude, that was sixth grade. What's going on?"

"I need to call in a favor. All my chips," Anthony said, pushing a large peach smoothie from Jamba Juice across the table.

David held his hand up and backed away. "Whoa. You need my kidney or something?"

"Can you go with Ty to pick out cakes tonight?"

An evening staring at pictures of cakes that all looked the

same? No way. "McKayla was terrible. I really didn't have any advantage over you in that game, even though Kurt couldn't play football to save his life," David said.

"Seriously, Beast. I can't go. It's just Sophie. She called to let me know her mom had an appointment with another client."

"So have Ty take her mom again. It makes way more sense. I am the last person a girl takes to an appointment with her wedding planner to pick out cakes." David grabbed the smoothie for good measure. Anthony owed it to him for asking him to go and expecting David would say yes.

"We both know Sophie well enough to know if I don't show up, she'll pull a few tricks of her own—like planning a wedding Ty's going to hate and not giving her the option to say no. Not that Ty would try. She already feels so beholden to Sophie for all the stuff she and her mom are hooking us up with. And I love Kim to death, but she's as spineless as her daughter." Anthony put his hands together in a prayer-like pose. "Come on. For Ty."

"Mrs. Daws raised three boys and Ty. I think she can take Sophie," David said, shaking his head and going for more smoothie. He needed to have it gone by the time Anthony realized David wouldn't give in.

"Her three boys *and daughter* are named after BYU football players. Clearly the woman can't say no either."

David sat back. "It's just a cake, Dreamy."

"I want Ty to have the best wedding she possibly can—I want it to be her dream, and even though Sophie's an evil mastermind, she's serving that up on a platter. Ty needs backup. She needs tough backup. Someone who can stand up against the steamroller that is Sophie Pope on a mission." Anthony leaned farther forward with every sentence of his speech.

"If it's that important, why don't you just man up and go? It can't be that bad."

"And have Sophie pouring on the charm right in front of Ty? Seriously, Beast, think about it. If I go, odds are heavy in favor of the whole thing ending in a disaster, and there goes my girl's perfect wedding. I'm asking you for a couple hours—for Ty. And besides, you already drank the smoothie. That's basically an agreement."

Okay, so Anthony made a good argument. And it wasn't a surprise that his superhero-like protective instincts had kicked in. His reaction to a creepy guy showing Ty the wrong kind of attention when they first started dating had been one of the tell-tale signs that Ty was more than just another woman to him.

Besides, David had seen Sophie on her tame setting around Anthony—the flash in her eyes at the concert said she'd take everything up to full throttle with Anthony on the line. It was all or nothing for her, and she wouldn't stop to think about Ty or her feelings. It wasn't exactly that Sophie didn't care how she treated other people—it was her don't-take-prisoners attitude of tackling goals. None of her friends doubted that Sophie would go far in life.

"Fine," he said. "For Ty. But you can't get out of this stuff forever, and you still owe me."

Anthony flashed his you-the-man grin and reached over to bump David's fist. "I'll make sure Mrs. Pope will be at the next appointment. Promise."

"You better."

David hit the library after classes, hoping to get a couple good hours of studying in before he had to meet Ty at his apartment to go to the cake place. It still surprised him that he'd agreed to Anthony's scheme. With any other guy, David would see right through it. But Anthony did it because he cared about Ty. And he was overprotective. David had witnessed that enough in action to believe it.

He opened up his e-mail before he got to his organic chemistry study guide. A message from his brother brought his day up quicker than anything else could. Some days he envied Noah.

Out on his mission, away from girls, baseball, school, everything. And though it pricked at David's pride to admit it, Noah was a much better missionary than David had been. More focused. Not worrying if his football scholarship would still be there, or if he'd be in good enough shape to play when he got back, or if he should've chosen baseball or gone on a mission at all.

David gobbled up his brother's letter, optimistic despite the fact that two investigators had backed out of baptismal dates. David's brow furrowed when he got to the last paragraph. "Jay e-mailed this week. First letter for a month or so, and it totally bowled me over. He's quitting baseball and putting off his mission. Probably indefinitely. Do you know what's going on with him? Maybe you could check it out for me."

Jay was Noah's best friend. Really, David's mom had raised six boys, since Jay had spent most of his waking—and a lot of his non-waking—hours at their house. Shamefully, David hadn't thought much about Jay since David's family moved to California right before Noah's mission. Where was Jay playing ball again? UVU? David would have to ask his mom.

He ignored his homework even longer to type back his response, promising Noah he'd figure out what was going on with Jay. By the time he finished writing and reread Noah's letter, the thought of helping out Ty for a couple hours didn't bother him as much anymore.

chapter four

THIS WAS RIDICULOUS. But Sophie could only grind her teeth together and walk up to Ty and David like she expected him. Oh, he was hot enough in his own right, with his short hair that always curled a bit on the ends. She wondered if, after BYU, he'd let it grow. She bet he could work the moppy hair well. He was tall, built like a football player should be. Toned arms, but not too beefy. Yeah, she'd admit to wondering how she would fit inside of those arms.

Except she aimed for the top. Anthony. She fought against asking why Anthony hadn't come. Instead of showing her discomfort by running her hands over her white jeans and straightening the mint peplum blouse, she took pride in knowing she looked perfect as she approached.

David's impressed expression said so too. She gave herself a mental high-five.

"And all this time I thought Ty was marrying Anthony ... you should have told me you changed your mind." Sophie set her black Valentino bag on the table and put a hand on her hip.

"Anthony has a big final he's studying for, so David came along to help instead." Ty flashed an innocent smile, eyes wide and all. Hmmm. Sophie had to give her some props for that.

Acting like nothing was going on. Well, Ty may have beaten Sophie for Anthony once, but not again.

"Hope you're not disappointed," David added with an I-know-what-you're-up-to smirk.

She touched his elbow, letting her fingers linger, biting her lip for the briefest moment. She leaned closer. "Not at all." She smirked back.

David let out a breath. "Hmm. That's good."

"I'll go get Genevieve. She e-mailed me some ideas for you this morning, and you're going to love her stuff," Sophie said, catching Ty watching them as she turned. Wouldn't it make Ty feel a lot better for that scene to be real? All things considered, David Savage would make a good boyfriend. Sophie's affections were just engaged elsewhere.

"Genevieve? You mean the owner of the shop?" Ty asked.

"Of course." Sophie tipped one shoulder up. "You hired the best." She walked away, her mind already spinning. She had to figure out a way to get Anthony to these appointments. The whole plan threatened to collapse around her ears at any moment. He got defensive when anyone attacked Ty. Unfortunately, Sophie had made that mistake and seen his reaction firsthand.

Besides, June would skin Sophie alive if she did something to upset one of the brides. The unwritten motto of June Pope weddings was to keep the bride happy whatever it took. Nothing came to Sophie before she made it to the silver "Employees Only" entrance to the kitchen. She took a deep breath and mentally added "figure out how to get Anthony to the appointments" to her to-do list.

She returned a few minutes later with the tall, auburn-haired owner of *For Richer & For Sugar*. Not many people knew about Genevieve's shop—yet. June had used her a lot since one of their regular caterers had referred her a few months before, and her work suited Ty perfectly. Great cake designs without too much fuss.

"Hi, Ty. I'm Genevieve." She took a seat across from Ty and set an iPad between them. "June had me add a few pins to your wedding Pinterest boards. Why don't you take a look and tell me how close it is to your idea of your dream wedding cake." She swiped across the screen a few times and pulled up the boards Sophie had created for them. David slumped in his seat.

Sophie hid her triumph. David was a football-and-pizza kind of guy. He stuck to video games and hanging out with his friends. This would be his first and last wedding planning appointment, and Anthony would be back in his proper place next to Ty—and back under Sophie's thumb—in no time.

"Okay." Ty brushed her fingers over the iPad, glancing over the cakes, her face glowing. "You're good."

"Sophie says your colors are blue and white?"

Ty reddened. "I know it seems silly, but it's Anthony. And it's me."

"It's your day. Nothing is silly," Sophie said, and the words surprised her. She meant them, like she did with every bride she worked with. She had to be careful of falling into this role and wanting to make Ty happy. It was one thing not to upset her. It was another to believe Ty would marry Anthony.

"What do you think of this one?" Genevieve tapped one of the cakes, and the picture took up the screen. Three tiers, alternating white and purple—"We'll do blue, of course. Tiffany blue? Royal blue?" Genevieve asked. "The burlap and ribbon sort of gives it a homier feel."

"I like it. It's perfect. Thanks," Ty added, genuinely, to Sophie.

The tiniest inkling of guilt tickled in Sophie's stomach. "You're welcome." Her gaze flickered to David. He watched her carefully, his expression filled with mirth. "You look bored, David. Gen? Do you mind if I get him some samples?"

Genevieve's eyes gleamed. "Of course not." She turned back to Ty. "That's how we keep the grooms entertained. You going to let him choose the flavor?" She winked.

David's face colored. "I'm actually the groom's best friend. He's inexcusably absent today."

Genevieve laughed it off. "Oh, I see. Well, help yourself. I want to show Ty a few more designs and talk to her more about what she wants specifically. It's the part of the appointment where most grooms fall asleep anyway." She and Ty went back to poring over the iPad as Sophie led David away.

They stepped up to a counter where one of Genevieve's employees served small squares of cake to three other couples. Good. Genevieve was getting popular, as she should.

"Hi," Sophie said to the employee nearest to her. "I'm Sophie, from June Pope's office. We need some samples."

"Of course."

Within a minute, a small tray with half a dozen different flavored cakes sat in front of them. "Let me know if there's anything specific you want to try." She hesitated only a second before going back to check on another couple near them.

Once David had his mouth full of Genevieve's signature dark chocolate cake, Sophie said, "Don't think I don't know what you're doing here."

He didn't even flinch. He took his time savoring the cake. Sophie tried not to approve of his apparent satisfaction with it. "Saying that you know what I'm doing means admitting to being up to something."

"I never hid the fact that I wasn't going to let him go without a fight. So why isn't Anthony here? Scared?" She slipped a bite of the white chocolate with raspberry swirls into her mouth and took her time using her lips to scrape it all off the fork. David's gaze strayed to her lips and stayed there.

"Yeah. Okay. He's scared you'll do something to hurt Ty. He thought he'd better avoid you." David took a deep breath and focused on the cakes, picking up the cheesecake drizzled with strawberry and chocolate sauces. Genevieve's cheesecake was a masterpiece. Excellent choice.

"It's not going to last. Sure, she knows football and she's

comfortable in a pair of jeans and a T-shirt, but that's not going to cut it when he's a pro football player. He needs someone who can take all the pressure of a celebrity lifestyle and still come away smiling. Someone strong enough to support him in that kind of thing. Someone who knows how to stand beside him and look good next to him."

David rolled his eyes. "Like Anthony cares one snot about that."

"Ha." Sophie shook her head. "He cares. All guys care what girls look like."

David paused with the last bite of the cheesecake hovering near his mouth. Sophie took the fork, her fingers brushing his, and guided it to her mouth. He swallowed along with her. Yeah. Mmmm, creamy and rich; just as great as ever.

"Well..." He cleared his throat and tore his gaze away from her lips again. "If that's true, why didn't he ever take it further with you?"

"I know broken, and it was written all over his face when I first met him. He needed time to heal before he was ready for anything serious. You don't go beating down his door and expect to accomplish anything. I was patient for a reason." She reached for the final sample, classic white wedding cake with cream cheese frosting. David grabbed her hand, stopping her from taking it. When she caught the pity in his expression, she wanted to snatch back her words for how much they said about her.

"I knew what I was doing with him. I'm actually pretty smart," she snapped, trying to cover her earlier moment of vulnerability. Especially when she recognized a voice she'd hoped never to hear again behind her, saying to one of the employees, "We're definitely not going with the dark chocolate. It's too bitter. What else do you have?"

David glanced that direction and chuckled. "Poor guy. Thinks he's going to have a say in all this."

Knowing her ex, Donavan... He probably had all the say. "Huh. Yeah," she said.

"You have crumbs all over your shirt," Donavan snapped, his voice clear above any of the other chatter. Like always. "Why would you wear a white shirt to pick out a wedding cake? What a stupid idea."

Sophie couldn't help her reaction, reaching down and flicking non-existent crumbs from her own white jeans. Come to think of it, it *was* kind of a bad idea to wear white around so much chocolate.

Even Genevieve and Ty looked up from their consultation at the table nearby, Genevieve scowling at the man interrupting the peace of her wedding bakery.

"What's that dude's problem?" David asked, his own expression pretty dark.

"He's probably just concerned for her. Doesn't want her to be embarrassed," Sophie said. She bit her tongue. Same lame excuses. They weren't true, so why did she even say it? Habit?

The slant of David's eyebrows deepened over his brown eyes. They snapped with anger, which intrigued Sophie. David, the knight-in-shining-armor type?

"You know that guy?" he muttered.

Donavan saved her the trouble of answering. "Soph? Sophie? What a coincidence."

She turned. She smoothed her shirt, checking for any signs of crumbs—none, *phew*—and ran her now-clammy hands over her jeans, giving herself away. She still cared about his approval, and she hated that part of herself.

"Hey. Hi. Donavan." *Stand tall. Be brave. Show him what he walked out on and how dumb he was for doing it.*

"Who's this?" Donavan reached for David's hand. It took David several seconds to extend his own and shake it—briefly. "That's crazy. Both of us getting married now, considering."

Oh, she hoped he didn't finish that thought. Not in front of David. She'd once cared too much about Donavan's opinion of her. The thought of David seeing her that weak made her skin crawl. She had to speak up to stop Donavan from going on.

She gestured at David. "We're just—"

David's hand slid around her waist and pulled her toward him so that she fit next to his hip, almost perfectly. "Oh, you're *that* Donavan," David said. "Yeah, I still can't believe it most days. Well, I mean, she told me no about twelve times, but she was too perfect to give up." He rubbed the side of her waist with his thumb. Something electric shot away from it. His touch? Or the way he defended her to Donavan?

Donavan snickered then wrinkled his eyebrows, confused that David was serious about it. Sophie pressed her lips together. Yeah. She'd do her part too.

"Well." She tilted her head toward David. "I'm too good for him, but twelve proposals? That'll wear a girl down." She gazed at David and remembered the words Ally had said so often after Donavan had left. *You are better than Donavan ever gave you credit for.* Sophie had started to believe it. And her mom had always said to own the room like everyone there wanted to be you. The dumbfounded expression on Donavan's face made the whole scene perfect.

He flashed a brief frown before a cross between a sneer and a smirk settled on his face. "Twelve, huh? Seems a bit desperate."

David chuckled. "Jealous much?" He dropped his hand and slid it into hers. "Well, see you around, Don. Or probably not." He led Sophie away, back toward the table where Ty and Genevieve sat, staring at them. "Hopefully not," he added in a stage whisper. A fit of giggles tried to get out of Sophie's chest. Donavan *hated* it when people shortened his name, and David had made him look like a fool. She would die to see Donavan's face right now, but she didn't look back. She never should have in the first place.

"What a jerk," David muttered when they approached the table.

Sophie's thoughts exactly. "Yeah."

Ty's eyes went straight to their hands. David didn't let go. "What's going on?" she asked.

"Oh, Sophie introduced me to her charming ex-boyfriend." He jerked his head back in Donavan's direction.

Ty laughed. She must know David well if that explanation covered it for her. "The guy who looks like he wants to knife you in the back?"

"Probably."

"How was the cake?" Ty rested her elbow on the table.

"You're never going to be able to decide. Maybe she can do three different flavors?" David suggested.

"You'll also be ordering sheet cakes to serve, right? You can have as many flavors as you want." Genevieve's face lit up with gratitude.

"Take one of everything." David rubbed his stomach with his free hand. Sophie wondered when he would let go of hers. Why hadn't she let go either? He turned to her. "Well, I'd better ride with you. It'll look stupid if I take off with another girl." He handed Ty his keys.

If Sophie rode alone with David, he might ask questions. He might keep holding her hand, though Sophie had no idea why she cared if he didn't. Or why she cared if he did. She didn't *not* like it. There was something to the comfortable way he'd acted around her, and she couldn't deny it flattered her that he'd stepped up to put Donavan in his place without knowing anything about the situation. She'd already broken up with Donavan by the time she moved in with Ally. In fact, Ally was the only one of her friends now who even knew about him and how many pieces he'd left Sophie in when he called off their engagement.

"Um. Okay." She picked up her purse. "Well, Ty. Call me if you need anything between now and meeting with the flower guy. And..." She'd written something else down earlier to check with Ty about... "Oh, uh, let me know when you guys settle on a date."

Ty studied Sophie, her face carefully devoid of any expression except for the slight dip of one corner of her lips. Disapproval? Probably. "Okay. Thanks, Sophie. This is great, by the way. All of it."

"You're welcome." Sophie needed to get out of there before Ty's gratitude guilted her too much. "See you later." She strode out of the shop, tugging David along behind her. She dropped his hand once they walked out of sight of the customers inside. Just to give her hands something to do, she rummaged for her phone in her purse.

"So what's Don's deal?" David asked, hurrying to keep up with her.

She glanced up at David as her fingers closed around her phone. "He hates that. People calling him Don."

"I figured." He offered her his fist to bump.

Sophie rolled her eyes but laughed with him anyway. He kept pulling it out of her. "What *was* that in there? You rescuing me?"

"Since when has Sophie Pope ever needed rescuing? You could have handled him on your own, right? He needed to be put in his place, and I really wanted to do it."

Sophie hesitated a step. She *could* have taken care of it herself. But she hadn't. She'd let David step in. "Of course I could have," she said in a rush. She turned her attention to her phone as they approached her 4Runner. Dang. No urgent e-mails or texts to answer. She'd give anything for a demanding bride right about now. Anything to keep from talking to David about Donavan. She held out her key and clicked the locks on the car.

"So who is he?" David opened the door but waited to get in until she had.

She dropped her useless phone into the cup holder in the middle console, daring it to ring with a wedding emergency. "The answer to that is obvious from the conversation we just had. Ex-boyfriend."

David settled in his seat with a, "Nice. Leather," and buckled his seatbelt. "He was more than an ex. Well, more than an ex-boyfriend. Ex-fiancé, right?"

She shrugged, focusing on starting the car to avoid talking about David's assumptions.

He reached over and rested his hand on her arm. "Sophie, is there something you want to tell me about your past?"

Sophie sucked in a breath. Because he touched her? Because she'd rather keep flirting with him than answer his questions? "Like what?" she said, irritated.

"Like that you were briefly committed to a mental asylum and that's where you met Don?"

She let out a laugh. "No. But okay, close enough."

"Well, it's the only explanation why a woman as smart as you would date a tool like him."

"Maybe." She focused on the road. Or maybe the only explanation was that she'd never gotten more than casual relationships with most other guys. Even Anthony had always kept things on the surface—going through the motions of a relationship but never really taking the big steps to make thing serious. She and Donavan had talked about marriage and their future and their dreams. It had seemed like the real deal. And she'd been stupid wrong.

"No matter what your motivation, this is nice what you're doing for Ty. Anthony appreciates it."

Sophie waved her hand, swatting his words away. "Quit trying to guilt me into giving up on Anthony. Anyway, doing his wedding is good publicity for my mom. If it happens."

David chuckled. "You don't know him as well as you think if you really believe he'd do anything to break Ty's heart. She's had him wrapped around her finger since he first met her. Nothing's going to come between them, not even a force like you."

Her heart fluttered at his wording. Her? A force? "Then maybe you don't know me as well as you thought you did."

David tilted his head and studied her. "I'm pretty sure I don't."

Thankfully, Sophie pulled up in front of his house. She didn't want to untangle that statement or David Savage and the surprising butterflies he made take off inside of her. The way he stood up for her tightened the link of friendship between them. After Ally, David and the other guys who lived with him and Anthony were her closest friends—but the scene in the cake shop and her and David's talk afterward shifted that friendship into more. And without Sophie's permission.

"So, should I expect to see you instead of Anthony when we pick out the flowers?" she asked.

"Do you *want* to see me instead?" David put his elbow on the console and leaned forward, scrutinizing and unsettling her.

If she kept laughing at him, it would encourage him to keep up this meaningless flirting that was starting to go to her head, but her amusement escaped anyway. "Keep wishing."

"FYI, even if you weren't out to ruin his relationship, Dreamy probably still wouldn't show up to any of this stuff." He pushed open the door and stepped out, then put his head back in. "Later, Sophie."

Sophie sat there watching him until he paused at his door and caught her. She grabbed her phone and jammed it to her ear, but he laughed anyway before he went inside.

She'd never made such a fool of herself—and that was unnerving, to say the least.

chapter five

SOPHIE LEANED through the doorway of the back room where the workers from Liz's Kitchen were busy drizzling triangles of cheesecake with Liz Allen's divine raspberries and cream sauce.

"You guys got any more chocolate-dipped strawberries? We're running low." She winked at the three girls.

"Coming up," one said, setting aside her pastry bag and opening a cooler.

Sophie stepped away and let the door swing shut behind her. June and Evan, the photographer, came to a halt in front of her. "Soph, I have three flower girls MIA, and we need to do pictures." June sighed.

Sophie's favorite duty at receptions. "I'm on it. I'll round them up." She handed her mini iPad to her mom.

Evan's gaze fell over Sophie. Admiring her pleated orange skirt and matching peep-toe heels? More likely the stretch of thigh between her knee and the hem. He raised his eyebrows. "Sophie? And kids?"

That stung more than if he'd said something like, "In those shoes?" which was what she usually heard.

"I leave it to Sophie when it comes to kids. She works some

kind of magic. Not sure how, since she's an only child." June had already started back toward the main room of the reception hall.

Sophie headed away too, not hearing Evan's retreating steps behind June until she'd taken half a dozen of her own. He hadn't asked her out since she'd turned him down at that first wedding —she could *not* go out with a guy who considered putting a suit coat on over his "Your Girlfriend Thinks I'm Hot" T-shirt dressy enough for weddings—but it hadn't stopped him from looking.

She paused as she stepped into one of the intersecting hallways. Three flower girls—two seven-year-olds and an eight-year-old. The younger ones were always harder to find since they found any off-limits room intriguing. But the older ones? Bride's room. Sophie would bet her closet full of shoes on it.

And when she came in view of the room, she softened her steps, needing to take a look before the girls realized she'd found them. She rested against the wall to the side of the door and tipped her head to the side, the sight that met her filling her with pleasure. Three girls in lacy, ruffled, adorably overdone fuchsia dresses twirling in front of the three-way mirror, lipstick streaked over their mouths and eye shadow up into their eyebrows.

"Oh, girls," she said, alerting them to her presence. They froze, looking at each other apprehensively. "This will never do." Three expressions fell in unison. The oldest one glanced in the mirror before turning back to Sophie.

"Nobody will let us wear makeup," she said, frowning.

"We want to look as pretty as Aunt Bridget." One of the seven-year-olds folded her arms, and Sophie got the impression she would have to drag her out.

"But you guys don't want to look prettier than Aunt Bridget, do you?" Sophie crouched down in front of them. "'Cause you guys are going to outshine her big time all dolled up the way you are now. How about you let me do your makeup, and you can look *almost* as pretty as Aunt Bridget."

The other seven-year-old clapped. "Really? We can wear makeup?"

That alone said that if Sophie did too much, it might upset their moms. "With such pretty faces, you won't need too much to make you all stunning." Three heads bobbed in unison. "Okay, I need names if we're going to be friends, right?" Sophie grabbed a makeup wipe from the table and set to work.

"Paisley." The seven-year-old Sophie had chosen to scrub first frowned as Sophie rubbed at her eyes.

"Kimber," the oldest said. She stood over Sophie's shoulder, running her fingers carefully over Sophie's curls as she watched.

"Emma," the third one said.

"And I'm Sophie," Sophie said, moving on to wipe off Emma's makeup. "The best flower girl makeup artist in town." The girls giggled. Within another few minutes, she had their faces squeaky clean again. Walking on her knees, Sophie kneeled back in front of Paisley and brushed a light coat of pale pink eye shadow over one of her eyes.

"Can you do my hair like yours, please?" Kimber asked.

She wore a flowered headband that held back a riot of blonde curls her mom must have worked at all morning. She might not like Sophie having to comb out half to pin Kimber's hair so that it hung in waves over one side.

"Let's make a deal," Sophie said, dusting Emma's closed eyes in two quick strokes. "First we do pictures because my mom is trying to find you girls so we can get that done. Then we'll come back here." And hopefully Kimber's mom wouldn't mind. "Now close your eyes." Two more swipes. She didn't wait for any other reaction than the careful nod the girl gave her. "Now blush and then we're off, okay?"

She barely dipped the brush into the blush, but made a show of spending time on the girls' cheeks with it. "Ta da!" She grabbed the girls' arms and pushed them in front of the mirrors. "Ooops. I wasn't careful enough. You three might be prettier than Aunt

Bridget." She faked a grimace, and the girls giggled. Her phone dinged in her pocket, but Sophie ignored it. In her book, little girls always came before needy brides or desperate boys.

"Ah-ha." A voice interrupted from the doorway. "So here you girls are."

One of the girls' mothers stood there. Kimber's, Sophie guessed, by the way the mom scrutinized the little girl.

"Don't they look so beautiful?" Sophie asked, tipping her head toward the wet wipes on the vanity behind her, a pile of them streaked heavily with makeup.

The woman pressed her fingers against her lips. "We'll have to make you stand in back so you don't outshine Bridget." She held up a finger and pretended to scold them all. More giggles. "Let's go." The woman ushered them out into the hall.

"How many little sisters do you have?" she asked Sophie in a low voice. "They probably adore you."

"None, actually." That compliment never got old.

"Mom?" Kimber tugged at her mom's arm. "She says that after the pictures she can fix my hair like hers."

The woman glanced at Sophie, who held her breath. "That would make you look so grown up, wouldn't it?" the mom said diplomatically, her lips drooping the slightest bit.

"Can I, Mom? Please? I want to look like an actress too."

"I can distract them afterward with something. She'll forget all about it," Sophie offered in a whisper.

The mom shook her head at Sophie before crouching in front of her daughter. "It's okay, as long as Miss Pope has time. Remember, today is Aunt Bridget's day, and we wouldn't want to get Miss Pope in trouble for not doing her job."

Kimber swung her head toward Sophie, already disappointed. "Oh. Yeah."

"You're in luck," Sophie said. "It just so happens that keeping *everybody* happy and having fun *is* my job."

The little girl threw her arms around Sophie's legs. "When I get married, I'm going to ask you to make everything pretty like you did for Aunt Bridget."

Sophie shared a look with the woman before planting a careful smooch on the girl's cheek. "I'll be there. Promise it won't be for a very, very long time."

Hands in his pockets, David hurried across the almost-deserted apartment complex parking lot in Orem. Most of the people in this complex were in church right now. Except for Jay Hunter. David had checked. Thanks to his mom, he had Jay's address. Hopefully he was at home. David had already sat through the first half of Jay's ward's sacrament meeting, hoping Jay would show and then ducking out when he didn't.

David knocked on the apartment door and took a couple steps back, rocking back and forth on his heels. He hadn't seen Jay in a long time. He didn't even know if his brother's friend would want to talk, and David had no reason for showing up except that Noah had asked him to.

The door opened. Jay stood at the door in a pair of basketball shorts and no shirt. His eyes were glazed over and tired. David checked his watch. One p.m.?

"Late night?" he asked.

"Beast?" Jay rubbed his eyes and leaned forward. "What're you doing here?"

"Thought I'd come catch up. How's it going?" He waited for Jay to invite him in, but he didn't, so he rocked back, giving Jay more space.

Jay surveyed him, squinting into the light behind David. "Are you my new home teacher or something? What're you dressed like that for?"

"Just came from church. Your ward, actually."

Jay looked at the floor and chuckled. "Should've seen this coming. Noah sent you, right? To check up on me."

"What can I say? Married people and missionaries. They think everyone should share in their joy." David grinned. "Believe me, personal experience right now."

"I heard something like that about Rocket." Jay supported himself against the doorframe, his eyes half closed. He inched the door shut, but David didn't give up so easily.

"So let's get together sometime. Play some catch or something. When you've ... rested up." David forced himself not to comment on Jay's disheveled state and the distinct smell of alcohol wafting off him.

"Don't worry about it. Tell Noah everything's fine. A mission just isn't me. Thanks for coming by." Jay softened his words with a halfhearted smile but didn't wait for a reply before he shut the door.

David should have known better than to think he could drop by and solve everything by the time he wrote another e-mail to Noah. He shook his head and took his time walking down the stairs and to his car. David would have to find a way to get Jay talking and figure out if his suspicions about what kept him up late and away from church and baseball were true.

David definitely had better things to worry about than another blind date that Ty had set up, but Juanita's was Juanita's. He didn't turn down invitations like that. Instead he grabbed another one of Ty's battered zucchini fries and stuffed it into his mouth.

"As if it's not bad enough when *he*," she jerked her thumb at Anthony, "steals my fries, you've got to do it too? What chance do I have?" She yanked them toward her and cradled them in her arms, one hand covering them. "Order your own, you two."

"Where would the fun be in that?" Anthony wrapped his arm around her and pulled her close, then reached under her hand and grabbed a fry, which came out mangled. He shoved it in his mouth anyway. Cardinal rule at Juanita's: Never waste food.

Ty's phone beeped, and she had to leave her fries unguarded to check the text. She glared at both David and Anthony. Anthony laughed and grabbed more fries, but David resisted.

"Looks like you're getting stood up," Ty said as she replied to the text.

"That's actually a relief," he said.

Ty chuckled. "Should we call Sophie?"

"That scene was for that creep she used to date, but it explains a lot about her." David sat back as their regular waitress, Lupe, set his double order of the enchiladas plus a club-sandwich combo in front of him. His mouth watered at the spicy chili scent mingling with the homey smell of cheddar and bacon.

"What do you mean?" Ty asked after Lupe set down her and Anthony's plates and walked away.

"He was the type of guy who wanted candy on his arm— someone who always looks and acts like she's supposed to," David said. *I know broken,* she'd said. He'd always put Sophie under the not-my-type category when it came to dating, but that didn't make her any less his friend. She and Ally spent almost as much time at his house as his roommates did—more time than Anthony lately. And he'd been to more than his fair share of parties and movie nights at their apartment. Thinking about how Donavan might have broken her made him clench his fists. That guy deserved a punch in the face for talking to any woman the way he had. David's mom hadn't just taught him that chocolate equaled forgiveness. She'd drilled it into her son how to treat girls—like queens.

"So you think she dresses the way she does to prove she's beautiful?" Anthony swirled a handful of fries in *Juanita's* spicy fry sauce.

David swallowed his bite of enchilada and chased the heat in his mouth with half his glass of water. "To prove she's worth dating."

Ty waved one of her zucchini fries around his face. "Stop. I can see it in your eyes, David. You think you're going to fix her."

He shook his head, startled. "Fix her? No. But she could use a friend in her life showing her that her self-worth isn't about how good she looks."

"And why would you be the 'friend' to do that?"

"I know she's after Anthony and that doesn't endear her to you, but she's still my friend." David sawed off another piece of enchilada. He glanced up at Anthony, who hadn't quit stuffing food in his mouth since it arrived, probably to keep himself out of the conversation.

"She's not going to appreciate finding out you're only spending time with her to boost her self-esteem." Ty sighed and picked up her fork.

Sophie needed someone, and David's innate chivalry pushed him to help. As a friend. "Why is it so bad that I want to make her feel better? Do you dislike her that much?" he asked, his fork screeching across the plate as he cut off another bite with more force than necessary.

Ty scowled. "No. That's not why. I'm defending Sophie. You shouldn't lead her on because you think she's some kind of project."

"She's not a project." That was true enough. The whole time they'd tried cakes, his thoughts had kept coming back to her lips. She'd look just as great in a pair of sweats and a T-shirt, maybe sitting on his couch, cuddled next to him ... She deserved to know that.

"So you like her?"

"Uh. No?"

She laughed. "Sure about that?"

"Cut him some slack, babe." Anthony broke into the conversation. "At least we could spend some Friday nights without him."

Ty looked between the two of them.

David bit back a smile. "Half of her wants to go on a double-date with Sophie so she can keep an eye on me. The other half doesn't want you anywhere near her."

"That's not true. Just be careful," Ty said.

"Don't worry about him," Anthony said. "His mom made sure we all turned out to be gentlemen."

"Well, it worked on you. Mostly," she said. "Thanks." He reached over and snagged another fry. "Hooligan."

Sophie rubbed her forehead as she flicked back and forth between the pictures sent to her by the wedding gown designers. All the boutiques and designers June used had offered last season's designs or display dresses that needed to be sold. It still didn't amount to much of a choice for Ty. If she cut out even one or two dresses, it would leave too few choices. But some of them weren't for Ty. Sophie shouldn't even be spending her time on this since finals started in two days and she should study, but she couldn't help it. Ty and Anthony weren't getting married, but *if* —big, big if—they did, Ty needed to look fabulous. So right now dresses ranked above her polishing her independent research project for one of her communications classes. And luckily, she loved choosing dresses for brides almost as much as she loved doing little girls' makeup.

"Whatchya doing?" Ally plopped onto the couch next to her.

"Wedding dresses."

"Mmmm. How's that whole thing going?"

"Anthony hasn't shown up once."

Ally snorted into her hand and turned it into a cough. "How long before he was on to you?"

"I'm guessing less than a minute." Sophie puffed out her cheeks then blew out a breath. "Ty brought her mom to the initial appointment and somehow managed to convince David to tag along to pick out cakes."

"Well, you win some, you lose some." Ally bent over Sophie's laptop. Sophie swallowed her desire to confess the sparks that had flown between her and David. In his words, she was a force. Forces didn't walk away from their goals because things went south.

"Let me see the pretty dresses." Ally ran the mouse over the first one and clicked it. "Ooooh, gorgeous!" she cooed over a drop-waist ball gown with a lace bodice.

"Uh-uh." Sophie shook her head. "Ty's too short for this dress. Her legs would disappear."

"I see." Ally moved on. "Oh, this one is fantastic. Not like you'd expect for a wedding dress. I love it."

Sophie spun the laptop back to her. For Ally, this dress would work. She would rock it. But Ty could never pull off the simple, dropped waist, Grecian style cap-sleeve.

"Again, she's too short for this." She clicked to a couple other pictures. "She needs something with a higher waist, something to lengthen her out. Maybe even a trumpet style or a sheath dress." Now Sophie really wanted to cut even more dresses, even if it meant leaving Ty with only three or four choices. She might have the same unskilled reaction as Ally—choosing a dress based on pictures and falling in love with something that would look terrible on her. Of course, Ty could always shop around on her own, but she'd never get anything as great as June Pope weddings could offer, especially for the price.

Ally sat back against the couch, studying Sophie.

"What?" Sophie asked. Why was Ally watching her like that, with hesitancy in her eyes and an almost frown?

"You're good at this. Knowing what will make someone look good."

"Your face is disagreeing with that compliment." Sophie squinted and leaned away.

"What if Ty wants one of those dresses?"

"I'm not going to show them to her."

Ally grabbed a pillow and picked at one of the buttons. "Is that fair? It's her wedding."

"She won't want to look like a dwarf in all her pictures." Sophie jabbed a finger at the Grecian dress on the screen.

"It's more about how she feels. You want to feel special on your wedding day. That's more important than how you look."

"How can you feel special in a dress that makes you look awful?" Sophie gaped at her roommate. "Ty doesn't have a lot of choices anyway. The designers are only offering a handful of designs for her dress budget, and if she wasn't marrying Anthony, she wouldn't get them at all. I'm putting in all this work for a wedding that's not going to happen, and *if* it does, I want it to reflect well on Mom. If I can make Ty look spectacular, isn't that a win for both of us?"

Ally stood and stepped away from the couch, heading for the kitchen. "You're the one who knows clothes." She waved her hand at Sophie and then buried her head in the fridge. "Did you throw out that pizza?"

Sophie turned her back on Ally. What was her deal? Yeah, Sophie loved clothes. She read about new styles and studied how to dress certain body types, how to highlight the best of her—and anyone else. She had an eye for it. Why did Ally have to get so defensive when Sophie used that knowledge to help people out?

"Yeah," she said, going back to the wedding dresses. "It was getting old."

"It'd only been in there a couple days." Ally shut the fridge with a snap and headed for the stairs with a sigh.

Not understanding why guilt tightened her chest, Sophie cleared her throat and minimized the window with all the dresses. Instead of thinking about Ty's, she'd drown her misunderstood self in an episode of *Say Yes to the Dress*. Criticizing other people's poor choices ought to chase away the unnecessary guilt. She could do homework later.

Sophie could not suppress her genuine delight as she pulled up in front of the Provo High School gym. Spring. A lot of people loved it because of graduation; for others it signaled the imminent arrival of summer. For her, prom, even if she had left high school five years before. Nowadays she got into it by volunteering with The Dream Dress Project, helping lower-income girls find a great dress among the many that got donated year after year. She'd started doing it during her senior year as penance for ruining Ciara Kelley's prom. Sophie shook the thought out of her head. She loved going to school after school, all over the valley, and picking out the perfect prom dress for girls. They always listened to her advice, and they always loved her choices. No one got all cranky when she told them a dress didn't flatter them and to try something else.

The first final she'd taken the day before had gone great and only served to increase her excitement. She *loved* this and all the weekends that would follow. She grabbed the bag of jewelry she and her mom had put together to donate and got out of the car, practically skipping to the already open doors. Corinne stood just inside, directing volunteers this way and that.

"Sophie!" She waved and hurried toward her. They hugged. Since Sophie had volunteered with Dream Dress for so long, she'd worked with the project's founder for years.

Sophie scanned the crowd when they broke apart. "Wow. Way more volunteers than last year."

Corinne bounced on her toes before grabbing one of Sophie's arms in excitement. "KSL is doing a piece today, and they got some local celebrities to come down and volunteer for a few things. One of their makeup girls is even going to do makeovers and give the girls tips."

Sophie froze as she caught sight of one particular local celebrity. "Rocket Rogers?" She arched an eyebrow at Corinne. What would Anthony have to do here?

Corinne's smile almost broke her cheeks. "Crazy, right? I couldn't believe it either when he showed up this morning. He's been hauling dresses inside and helping set up. He's going to stick around and sign a few autographs."

Sophie pushed her hair back off her face and frowned. She looked forward to this day all year, but now that Anthony had come without Ty, she had a chance to get her plan in motion.

"What's wrong?" Corinne asked.

Sophie wiped the expression off her face. She was Sophie Pope, after all. She'd figure out a way to make it work. Maybe she could get Anthony to spend some time with the girls she coached and hand out some compliments. They'd probably like that.

"Sophie?"

Anthony's voice tripped her out of her thoughts. He stood in front of her, balancing several garment bags over one arm.

"You guys know each other?" Corinne gaped, her cheeks flushed. Married with two kids of her own, and Rocket had her acting like a high school girl.

"Yep." Sophie turned her charm up full blast. "If I'd known you wanted him around, I could have brought him a couple years ago. Showed up at a party Ally threw right after I moved in and hasn't been able to stay away since."

Anthony laughed and glanced at Sophie. "Until recently," he said to Corinne. "I got engaged a couple weeks ago."

He didn't act embarrassed to stand so close to Sophie, like he had every time she'd tried to talk to him at parties or other gatherings since things got serious with Ty. The answer hit her like a ton of bricks. Ty must have told him about the thing with David, and she must have read way more into it than the innocent scene of David putting Donavan in his place.

"Congratulations," Corinne said.

"Thanks." Anthony peered at Sophie. "What are you doing here?"

Corinne answered for Sophie, placing a hand on her shoulder and drawing her close. "Sophie's volunteered with us since almost the beginning. The girls always love her, and she's so great at this," she gushed.

Sophie had to look away from his scrutinizing gaze. What did he think about her volunteering?

"That's awesome, Soph."

Sophie blinked at him, surprised he'd used her nickname for the first time since he started dating Ty. He'd kept his distance from her for a while. Why the sudden friendship? Because of David?

"Thanks." She took a moment to savor the compliment then caught her reflection in one of the nearby mirrors as Corinne walked away with her. Plain-Jane skinny jeans and a flowing, yellow shirt. She'd worn a pair of flats since she'd be on her feet well into the evening. She'd chosen great clothes—she always did —but not the best outfit to flatter her. Not the outfit she would've chosen if she'd known Anthony would show up. Sophie stopped at her booth, which had mirrors and a garment rack Corinne always set up for Sophie and the other coaches who volunteered. Was it dressing down that finally got Anthony's attention? He liked that about Ty. Huh. Well, it was something to think about.

One of the first girls through the door a half hour later waved and rushed over to Sophie as soon as she came in. "Good, you're here!"

Sophie gave the girl a half hug. "Hey there, Alexa. Back again?"

Alexa pulled her stick-straight, dark blonde hair off her shoulders. At least it looked healthier now than it had two years ago, when she'd first showed up as a sophomore and Corinne sent her to Sophie's booth.

"Senior year," Alexa said, her hazel eyes sparkling. She'd toned down her makeup from last year, though all Sophie had said was, "Don't hide those gorgeous eyes behind all that eyeliner."

"Well, we better find you something amazing." Sophie examined the rack. She didn't have to look twice. The column-style dress she'd grabbed earlier fit Alexa perfectly. It would accentuate her height, and the ruched bodice and cinched waist would create curves where Alexa had none. With her fair skin and cool skin tone, the hot pink would stand out.

Alexa shoved her hands in her pockets and scrunched her shoulders together. At almost six feet, the girl was always trying to appear smaller, even though for two years Sophie had encouraged her to work her height. Alexa had added Sophie on Facebook the same day Sophie had chosen her first dress for the Dream Dress Project, and Sophie had witnessed Alexa growing more confident over the last two years.

"It's bright, Sophie," she said.

Sophie wiggled the dress in front of her. "And you're going to look great. You trust me, right?"

Alexa allowed a smile. "Of course."

"Go put it on. See what you think." Sophie shoved the dress at her and pointed to the dressing rooms, a section of the gym partitioned off with office cubicles. When Alexa returned a few minutes later, Sophie put her hands on her shoulders and stood Alexa right in front of the mirror.

"There's only one thing missing," she said with a wink.

"What?"

Sophie pulled back Alexa's shoulders, straightening her out to several inches taller than her. The curves appeared. "See how great you look?" Sophie said. "I've told you this a million times. Walk in like you—"

"Own the room," Alexa finished with an *I-got-this* head bob. Sophie dropped her hands. "Well?"

"I'm hot."

"What was that?" Sophie cupped a hand around her ear.

"I'm *super hot*."

"You better believe it." Sophie wrapped her arms around Alexa and caught Anthony watching her from the middle of the room, wearing that same scrutinizing expression.

She started to analyze it and stopped herself. Forget it. Today was her day. No. Today was Alexa's day, and hopefully at least twenty other girls' day. And Sophie meant to make it fantastic.

chapter six

DAVID SHOVED his phone in his pocket and slumped against the side of his house. If he thought he could make it past all those people to his bedroom so he could think in peace, he might go for it. But he never would. He should forget the call and go inside and try to have fun, despite the options crowding his head. With finals and graduation looming, he needed to relax like everyone else.

This wasn't the first time he'd gotten a call from Clint Parry, a scout with the Atlanta Braves. He'd talked to David his senior year of high school, but the choice to come play football for BYU, with Anthony, had been an easy one then. Now, after three more calls in almost as many years, the decision had gotten a lot harder.

And then there was the situation with Jay. David had texted him all week, but Jay kept blowing him off, refusing to get together with him. David fingered his phone and frowned at it. Should he try again?

"You look like somebody stole your best friend."

David looked up. Sophie walked up the sidewalk, dressed down by her standards. She wasn't even wearing heels. He furrowed his brow. Was something wrong with her? It wasn't like her to show up at one of their parties in anything other than a short skirt or something fancy.

"Oh, wait," she went on. "Somebody is." She winked.

He couldn't help studying her. Even though she smiled—and looked genuine about it instead of manipulating—something had to be going on.

"What?" she asked when he didn't answer.

He shook himself out of it. "Nothing. What's up?"

She dropped onto the front step and sighed, though it sounded more content than anything else. "I had a long day. A good day, but long, and my feet are killing me."

He sat down next to her without thinking about it. "Doing what?"

She stared at him for several seconds, her head tipped to one side and her eyes cautious. "You first. What's with your lost-puppy look?"

He hesitated. Sophie wasn't the first person who came to mind when he thought of confiding in someone, but she was here. And he'd decided to take her seriously. Treat her like a real friend should instead of dismissing her as a fangirl.

"I got a call from a baseball scout. Asking me to consider signing with their team." He didn't need to weigh her down with his troubles with Jay.

The news startled Sophie, like it did most people. "Baseball?"

He chuckled and picked up a nearby stick, tapping the steps with it. "Yeah. I played in high school and got a couple offers then, but I wanted to play football."

"Have you even played the last four years?" she asked.

Sure, when someone put it that way, it sounded like a long shot. "Not competitively, no. But it's not unheard of for an athlete to switch sports after college. I've got a shot, or he wouldn't call."

"But ... you're going to get drafted to play football now, right?" She rested her head against the rail and closed her eyes, looking exhausted instead of confused, as her tone suggested.

He watched her lift one of her legs and rest her ankle on her knee, rubbing her calf. "Maybe." He'd seen the same website Ty had. It called him an "eventual starter," but you never knew. Same with baseball. Just because a scout called didn't make David a superstar. So what did he want to do? Give baseball another chance? It would be an incredible challenge to make it to a professional level. He liked challenges. Sophie was a case in point.

She opened her eyes. "Why do you say it like that?"

He tapped her leg. "Give me that." She complied without hesitation and lifted her leg into his lap for him to massage. "Maybe I'll get drafted and never do a thing. It happens when athletes go pro. I know plenty."

Her shoulders relaxed, and her eyes drifted closed again. "So you've got a better chance in baseball."

"Not necessarily. Maybe I want to try that now ... but I love football, so who knows? Okay, now you."

She pulled her leg away and lifted the other. She seemed so ... real right now. Not some flirt who only cared about dating the hottest guy in the room. Maybe because she trusted him after the thing with her ex?

"I got to boss around a bunch of high school girls today."

He laughed. "You would enjoy something like that."

She grinned back. "I helped them find prom dresses."

"I bet you're good at that."

"I am. That feels amazing. You going to do my feet next?"

"It's going to cost you."

She opened her eyes and scrutinized him. "What do you want?"

"Another one of those sample trays from that cake shop we went to the other day."

"Done."

"That was easy. I should've gone for entire cakes." He slid his hand down her calf and slipped her shoe off. Sophie froze, and when David looked up to see why, he caught her staring at him, her breath held. "What?" he asked.

She shook her head. "Nothing." She closed her eyes again, but a faint blush rose to her cheeks.

He looked at his hands, encasing her foot, which was pretty soft as far as feet went. He moved his fingers and thumb in circles around the pads of her toes, and she relaxed. They sat silently together while he worked.

"Beast?" Anthony's voice interrupted. He pushed open the screen door. "What's keeping you—" He stopped in the doorway.

Sophie's eyes flashed open. She yanked her foot back. "Hey."

A grin slowly spread over Anthony's face as he took in the situation. "Hey, guys."

"Hi." David wished Sophie would give him back her foot to rub. Had the incident at the cake shop made him possessive of her? Or was it because she'd chased Anthony for two years and never looked twice at David until now?

"What's up?" he asked.

"Uh, nothing. Checking what that phone call was all about, but we can chat later." Anthony closed the screen door and disappeared back into the house.

Sophie pushed herself to her feet. "I better go find Ally. She's here, right?"

"Yeah, I think so. I saw her earlier."

Sophie opened the screen door and hesitated before going inside. A moment later the door shut behind her. He sat there for several minutes, wondering about what had just happened between them. He wanted more moments like that with … someone. Flirting. But easy stuff and no games. So different from his two dates with Katie. He'd pegged Sophie as the demanding one, but every interaction between them had been simple, like just now. Friendly and nice. Not that he expected anything serious out of a relationship with Sophie. He didn't picture her as the marrying type.

He got up and went inside. It didn't surprise him to find Sophie and Ally sitting on the couch with Anthony. It did surprise him that Sophie sat a couple feet away as opposed to attached to Anthony's side, especially since Ty hadn't shown up yet. It also surprised him that they were joking around, and Anthony sat back against the couch, his expression relaxed. Had Sophie gotten to him somehow?

David stood at the door, not sure what to do. Did Anthony need rescuing? Or was David making up excuses to spend more time with Sophie? He strode over there anyway.

"I rub her legs and everything, and still she deserts me for you. I don't get it." He stood over both of them, hands in his pockets, eye-brows arched.

"I keep hoping you'll get the hint one of these times," Sophie countered. That was more like the Sophie he knew, knowing no woman in the room looked better than her.

David wiggled down into the space between them, pushing Anthony into the arm of the couch and pressing Sophie up against himself. "Not likely. I'm concerned that since you only let me rub one of your feet, you're going to try and get out of paying me that full tray of samples."

"You only did half the work." She wouldn't look at him and instead studied the room, appearing uninterested in his attempts to get her attention back on him.

He put his arm along the top of the couch and leaned over so his lips almost grazed her cheek when he spoke. "And whose fault is that?" He pulled back a little. Enough to gauge his effect on her. She played it cool with her expression, but her bright eyes and parted lips betrayed her. When his eyes strayed to her lips, she closed them.

She shrugged and didn't answer.

He wouldn't give up those cakes easily. "Then I guess you can eat the other half. Or let me finish. Your choice."

Sophie blushed. David didn't see that often. Whatever she planned on saying, however, got interrupted by Ty's arrival at the door and Anthony jumping off the couch to go and greet her. Sophie's gaze followed him and, in consequence, so did David's. When Ty caught sight of him and Sophie cozied up on the couch, her lips curved down in disapproval that disappeared when Anthony caught her up in a hug.

Ty had dragged her feet at every mention of the possibility of Sophie and David—and at this juncture it was just flirting. David would distract Sophie from her plan to steal Anthony. He had expected Ty to approve of that plan wholeheartedly.

Annoyed with everything from Ty to himself to Sophie, he pulled his arm back. "I'm headed to the kitchen for food." He stood before he realized he should offer something to Sophie. "Want me to get you anything?" He'd already moved away from the couch, not waiting for her to answer.

Her eyebrows furrowed before she wiped the expression off and lifted her chin. "No, thanks."

David shoved his hands in his pockets. What a great night. First the baseball call, then failing at flirting with Sophie. He should've stayed outside.

The second Ally and Sophie met back at their house after the party, Ally pointed a finger at her roommate and commanded, "Spill it."

Since Sophie had had most of the party to prepare for this onslaught, she waved Ally off without a second thought. "About what?"

Ally put her hands on her hips and shook her head, a sly smirk on her face. "Uh-uh. No acting with me. You and David. Sparks." She made an explosion sound and threw her arms out. "Right? What's up?"

Sophie folded her arms and rested against the back of their couch. "Flirting. Ever heard of it?"

Ally shoved her over the back of the couch. Sophie righted

herself and watched Ally march around the couch and sit next to her. Right next to her. Head on her shoulder, hand caressing Sophie's arm.

"What are you doing?" she asked, fighting laughter.

Ally batted her eyes. "This is you flirting. That was *not* what was happening with David. You were blushing and swallowing and looking away. He had you flustered!"

Ally had that part right. Every time she talked to him since the cake shop he shook something up inside of her. He looked at her differently. Not critical, like Donavan. And not like she was only good for kissing, like a million other guys she'd dated. She couldn't figure it out. When he ran his fingers along her calf, slipped her shoe off, and cradled her foot like Prince Charming trying the glass slipper on Cinderella, she'd thought her heart might leap out and take a lap around the house.

She couldn't lie to herself. Nothing even remotely close to excitement and giddiness had ever happened during her most heated kisses with Anthony. Ever.

"Sophie?"

She blinked and noticed Ally swirling her fingers in front of Sophie's face. "Yeah. That look. Smitten is what I'd call it."

Sophie pushed Ally's fingers away. "You've known me awhile, and when have I ever been smitten with anyone?"

"I know." Ally did something that might be called a shimmy with her shoulders. "This is new. And exciting, right?"

"You seem to be the excited one."

Ally took Sophie's hands in hers and held them close. "Soph. You never acted like this with Anthony. Not the first time you guys kissed. Not even when you got back together the first time he broke up with you."

Sophie couldn't deny that. Her feelings in those moments, like winning him back after he'd started dating other girls— multiple times—or when they kissed, had been about triumph. Nothing like the rush of warmth when David had leaned over and his lips had nearly brushed her cheek.

She sighed. "Okay. So? What do you want me to do about it?"

"Go after David, dummy."

Sophie shook her head. "To him I'm another one of *those* girls after Rocket. He's watched me throw myself at Anthony. He probably thinks I'm pathetic."

Ally slapped her forehead and slumped against the other side of the couch. "How can someone as gorgeous as you be so insecure?"

"Because that's exactly it. All I am is a pretty face."

"It sounded like he thought of you as more than a pretty face when he confided his hopes and dreams for the future to you. That sounded like a guy who thought of you as a friend."

"Eavesdropper!" Sophie accused with a burst of laughter.

"Maybe," Ally admitted shamelessly. "You've never worried about what David thought of you before—and he's been your friend for a while. So don't start now."

"Okay then, what do you suggest?"

"This plan of going after Anthony is working pretty well so far. Why give it up?" Ally wiggled her eyebrows. "But don't forget his cakes."

chapter seven

SOPHIE HAD Ty down on her schedule to try on dresses at ten. She flipped through the binder one last time, familiarizing herself with the choices. What should she expect from a woman who wore jeans from Old Navy and owned more T-shirts than Sophie could comprehend?

Ty showing up with an entourage wasn't what Sophie had in mind, even if both David and Anthony were part of that entourage.

Ty must have caught Sophie's surprise as she, her roommate, the two guys, and her mom came through the door of June's offices.

"Sorry. I hope this wasn't too many. Rosie and the guys insisted they come. My mom is a given, right?" Ty waved toward Kim.

Sophie moved away from the reception desk, where she'd been waiting. "The *guys* insisted?" she questioned.

Ty cast a troubled glance over David before turning back to Sophie. "It doesn't count as Anthony seeing my dress if I don't tell him which one I decide on, right?"

"Not if you don't want it to," Sophie said, but she wondered more about why Ty cared that David had tagged along. "Follow me." She headed back to the office her mom had converted into a dressing room for the brides lucky enough to have designers bringing them dresses. "There's plenty of room for everyone." She opened the door and ushered them inside. Two big white couches with pale blue pinstripes sat at angles to each other facing a wide, three-way mirror and a pedestal. The thick, pale blue carpet and wispy white curtains gave the room a summery feel that most brides loved.

"I'll be right there." Sophie pointed to the wall on the left, where twelve dresses hung. "I'll send Jessica in to start helping you with the dresses." She shut the door behind her and headed for the break room, where she'd last seen Jessica, and where the box of sample cakes she'd picked up for David waited.

"Is Ty ready?" Jessica asked, taking one last hurried sip of her soda.

"Yep. I'll be right behind you," Sophie called as Jessica slipped from the room. She reached into the fridge and grabbed the box before heading back down the hall. So David had insisted on coming even though Anthony had shown up to support his fiancée. Had he come to run interference between her and Anthony or because he felt the same sparks Sophie did? And what was with the flutter in her chest? Guys never made Sophie nervous, even guys that came to her rescue or rubbed her feet. She took a breath. She was in charge here. If something was happening between her and David, it would happen because she said it could.

Ty was already in the changing room with Jessica when Sophie came back in. Rosie and Ty's mom chatted on one couch while the guys looked out of place on the other. Sophie set the box down on the dark brown coffee table in front of them.

"Technically these are for David, but since he didn't earn all of them, he'll have to share," she announced as she opened the top of the box to reveal two dozen bite-sized cakes in tiny white cupcake liners. "And it wouldn't hurt for you to try a few, Anthony, since Ty still hasn't made the final decision for the cake."

David dove toward them, cutting Anthony off. "You wish," he muttered. He hovered over the box. "I told you I would earn the rest when you gave me a chance," he protested. He gave her a full look, his eyes sweeping down her figure. She didn't miss the slight frown when he surveyed her skirt. She let her fingers graze the gray lace that lay over the gathered skirt of the same color underneath. It had an honored place in the forefront of her closet, with all her favorite clothes. The day she'd seen it in the store six months ago, the outfit possibilities had exploded in her mind. She'd made it work dressed up and dressed down. Sure, her mom had grimaced at its length—she preferred Sophie to wear skirts closer to her knee in the office. But Sophie loved clothes and loved outfit possibilities. David's appraisal of her reminded her of Donavan and the fact that he had critiqued everything she ever wore, good or bad. She pushed it all aside. She was past the point in her life where she worried about what a guy thought about how she dressed. She made her clothing choices now based on what she loved wearing.

She leaned over toward him, maneuvering as close to him as she dared with three onlookers. "Don't worry. I know the owner pretty well. I bet I can get more."

He held her gaze. The genuine enjoyment and interest in his expression made her knees wobble. "If you promise."

Maybe she'd imagined the disapproving frown. He cupped her elbow with his hand, and Sophie wanted him to do that thing where he wrapped his arms around her waist and pulled her close like he had at the cake shop, but that wouldn't be professional. June wouldn't like Sophie giving the impression that her employees flirted with the clients' entourage.

"Promise," she said.

He didn't let go of her arm yet, though. "Anthony showed me pictures from that dress thing you did this weekend. It looked like you had a lot of fun. The girls too. Bet they loved your expertise."

Okay, wow. That melt-her-insides grin and him asking her

about and complimenting her on this thing she lived for every spring? She should back away before she fell all over him. "You mean my bossiness?" she asked. Good. She sounded calm and indifferent there.

"We watched the piece KSL did, you know, since Anthony was in it." He glanced away, and she wondered if maybe he watched it to see her too. Was he embarrassed? "One girl couldn't stop saying how great you were. Have you seen it?"

"No, but maybe I should," Sophie said. The nerves in her chest had shifted into something warm and melty. This sort of thing had never happened to her before. Not even with Donavan. Weren't flirting and kissing and the adrenaline that came with going out with a good-looking guy the feelings girls talked about when they said they were in love?

"Well, here I am," Ty announced, interrupting.

Sophie whirled around. It was as she'd feared. Ty had chosen the Grecian dress. It shouldn't have surprised Sophie that laid-back, sports-loving Ty would go for the simple yet lacy and feminine one. Sophie had brought all the dresses because part of her agreed with Ally about how important it was for Ty to feel special on her wedding day.

And yes. Sophie had given up on winning Anthony over. Ally's observations, as well as her own, had shown Sophie that what she'd never really had with Anthony had never really been enough. The last few moments with David, save for her fleeting reservations about his judgments, has surpassed any moment she'd ever had with Anthony. She wanted more of that.

That meant making Ty's wedding day spectacular. But helping Alexa and the other girls with their prom dresses on Saturday had reminded Sophie how she could be right and so could Ally. Ty could look great *and* feel great if she chose the right dress. June let Sophie take care of the dresses with clients more often than not in the past year. Sophie knew wedding dresses.

"You look like a princess." Ty's mom interrupted Sophie's mulling. Sophie grimaced at the enthusiastic response.

"Don't fall in love with the very first dress," she scolded mildly, striding toward the pedestal where Jessica arranged the train. Sophie scrambled with how to talk Ty down from this dress without hurting her as she watched Ty gaze at herself in the mirrors with a far-off look. "This is a great, elegant dress that a lot of girls love, but we have quite a few that are going to make you look spectacular."

Sophie studied the crowd on the couches, searching faces for anyone who might support her position that this dress made Ty look like a hobbit playing dress-up. There. Forced approval filled Rosie's hesitant expression. Sophie jumped on it.

"What do you think, Rosie?"

"It's great."

Well, that was a disappointment. But to Sophie's surprise, Ty snapped out of her daydream and frowned at Rosie in the reflection before twisting to look at her, the light skirt fluttering and settling in an annoyingly attractive way.

"You don't like it," Ty accused.

Rosie shook her head. "It's so pretty, Ty. It's just the waist emphasizes the wrong places on you..."

Sophie hoped Ty understood what Sophie and Rosie both thought. *You look so small.*

"Let's try another one," Sophie said. She prided herself on keeping the brides happy, especially after less-than-enthusiastic comments and in bad dresses. "We can come back to this one if you want."

Ty now studied herself critically in the mirror. A tiny bit of guilt sparked in Sophie's stomach for causing that. Ignoring the feeling, she swept across the room and grabbed a lace trumpet-style dress Ty would shine in. It had a lot of the same elements as the Grecian one—simple, too, with the same long, draped skirt —but this one had a ribbon around the upper part of the waist, which would make Ty seem taller. It had a lace overlay that added femininity, and the way the skirt flared at mid-thigh would flatter Ty's slender waist and hips.

Though Ty walked out more subdued, her face lit up when she saw herself in the mirror. Sophie almost clapped in triumph.

"I look ... tall." She twirled for her audience. Sophie turned with her, surveying them.

Her mom stood and held her hands over her chest. Her nostalgic smile and shimmering eyes said that Kim Daws pictured a much younger version of Ty right now. "I'm so glad I'm not the one who has to choose. You look breathtaking, Ty," Kim said.

Sophie's gaze slid over David—she couldn't help at least peeking—on to Anthony. He grinned, the best reaction they'd get from the guys, so Sophie swung her attention to Rosie, whose opinion mattered to Ty.

"Perfect." Rosie nodded once.

Ty's subdued attitude dropped away, and she admired herself again with more enthusiasm. Sophie had never noticed this part of Ty's personality before, not that they'd gotten to know each other well at all over the past six months. The others' opinions mattered to her a lot. That surprised Sophie. Ty had swept into Anthony's life with so much confidence. Sophie still remembered the first night she'd seen Ty with Anthony. She'd come to a party at Anthony and David's. Sophie had been easing Anthony into the idea of them getting back together, and she'd had a plan for making it last that time. But he'd left her in the kitchen to greet Ty when she arrived. Sophie had expected him to come back—maybe not that night specifically, but sometime soon. And even though he'd called and asked Sophie out a few days later, he'd never really come back to her. He'd been Ty's from pretty much that moment on.

If Ty made Anthony feel nice and special and perfect inside, then maybe she really deserved him. Maybe that's exactly what Sophie wanted. Someone who could sit and stare at her the way Anthony stared at Ty right now, with a look that spoke volumes about how it didn't matter to him which dress Ty picked. She was all he could see.

Sophie shook herself from the reverie that the moment had created. "Okay, no falling for the second one either. You've got to try on at least a few more," she encouraged. "If you like this one, I have another one you're going to love."

Ty giggled and swirled the skirt back and forth, transfixed by the image of herself in the mirror. "You do seem to know what you're doing." She cast a look at Sophie over her shoulder, a mixture of confusion and approval. "You're good at this."

"Thanks." Sophie ignored the surprise in Ty's observation and headed to the rack for another dress—a much better dress. Modified boat neck, a line of flowers marking the high waist and a flowing, tulle skirt. If Sophie could choose a dress for Ty, she would choose this one. As soon as Sophie held it up, Ty waved her hands excitedly and reached for it.

"Ten bucks says this is the one," Sophie whispered to David as she passed.

"Think you're that good?"

"I know I am." She swung her hips ever so slightly as she strode past and ushered Ty back into the dressing room.

Ty didn't even glimpse in the mirror when she came out this time. Her whole face glowed. Sophie tilted an eyebrow at David, wishing she could say told you so.

He shook his head at her.

Sophie bent to straighten out the skirt around the pedestal. "This is a dress by a local designer, Jovi Roy, and she's fantastic."

Ty twirled around and around in front of the mirror. "I can't believe how amazing it looks." She halted and faced Sophie. "Are you sure this is in the price range we talked about?"

Sophie didn't let the lapse in trust bother her. "Cross my heart."

Ty's dreamy expression reappeared, and she did another twirl. Twirls. Sure signs that the bride had fallen madly, deeply in love with her dress. "Wow," Ty whispered to herself. It didn't surprise

Sophie that Ty didn't bother asking for second opinions either. She'd hear high praise for it if she did. Sophie saw it on all their faces.

She made Ty try on all the dresses, but none of them elicited the joyful response Jovi's dress had. Sophie was on her way to collect her ten dollars from David when Ty asked to try on the first one again.

"What?" Sophie blinked at her.

"Do you mind? It's so elegant, and I kind of looked like a model ... I want to try it on again. To make sure."

Sophie had half a mind to say no, but she snapped out of it. Ty would see that dress on herself and realize which one would make her stunning. "Of course."

Except she got all giggly again when she came out and admired her reflection. "I could just picture myself with like a Roaring Twenties kind of hairstyle. I still like it." She sighed.

"Better than Jovi's dress?" Sophie asked.

Ty shrugged. "I look different in this one, but it *feels* like the kind of dress a girl like me would get married in."

"As your wedding planner, and someone who is frankly good at what she does, I have to say the other one compliments you more."

"I'm sure you're right." Ty sighed. "But I let people tell me what to do a lot, and I've had a hard time speaking my mind when I thought differently from someone else. But this is my wedding. You can send all the others back, or whatever you do, but I can't choose between this one and the other one today."

Sophie didn't want to give in, but Ally's niggling words about it being Ty's day kept shoving their way through Sophie's better sense. "Fair enough," she conceded. "You don't have to decide today."

"Thanks." Ty stepped off the pedestal. "Rosie? Did you get pictures of me in both? I'm going to have to stare at them for a while."

"Yep." Rosie waved her phone around.

Ty gazed into the mirror one more time. "I really like this one," she whispered before she followed Jessica back into the dressing room. Sophie scowled at the door with her arms folded.

"Looks like you're on your way to losing ten bucks." David's voice surprised her. She jumped and turned her scowl on him.

"No way. She'll see the pictures and make the right decision —the dress that looks best on her. Jovi's dress," she replied in a low voice, moving away from the dressing room. Her gaze darted over to the others, who stood in front of one of the couches, discussing how Ty looked in the dresses. Anthony and Kim seemed in favor of all of them.

"And what if she doesn't?" David challenged, following her.

She met the challenge with a glare. "She won't."

He smirked but didn't answer, although she read *we'll see* plainly in his eyes.

She couldn't help adding, "If you talk her into that first dress, you'll be sorry."

He held up his hands. "I'll play fair. Promise. You're right that she looks awesome in the other one. I just know Ty."

His praise started dissolving her insides. Out of habit—and for her protection—her flirting instincts kicked in. She sidled closer and gripped his arm, lowering her voice. "And I know brides."

When June came back to the office after an appointment, Sophie was updating Ty and Anthony's binder in her office. June walked straight to the desk and peered over her shoulder, flipping through the pages to check out the plans they'd finalized and which ones still needed decisions. She *hmmm*-ed and nodded her approval over it. Sophie had taken over this wedding, except where she needed June for her connections. Putting the rest of the wedding together in just over forty days would take a lot of work. Ty and Anthony had to choose a sooner date, rather than later, to keep the costs low. The reception hall they'd chosen had a date coming up that they wanted filled and would give it to June at a steeply discounted rate in order to get something booked. Her mom had still swallowed some of the cost, and Sophie worked hard to make that up to her. It'd been her pushing in the first place that got Ty and Anthony the rock-bottom price June had given them.

"I'm very impressed," June said, coming to the last page—the dresses. She patted Sophie's hand before looking back down. "That PR degree is going to go to waste with you working here." She winked. "This is perfect," she said, tapping the Jovi Roy dress, and turned to the last page. "But ... this dress is all wrong for Ty." She frowned.

Sophie sighed and slumped into the desk chair. "I know. She liked the simplicity of it. Its elegance. I told her she didn't have to choose today, and everyone agrees she looks better in Jovi's dress. Ty's a people pleaser. She'll go with that one in the end."

June perched on the desk. "Brides will go their own way once in a while, no matter what we say."

Ty had said something about letting people walk all over her. What if this time, of all times, she chose to stand up just for the sake of doing so? Sophie couldn't let her do that when Jovi's dress made her breathtaking.

"Not if I can help it," Sophie said. "Jovi's dress is stunning on her, and I'd hate for the other one to overshadow her on her big day."

June chuckled. "Nothing can overshadow a bride on her wedding day. Not in one of my—excuse me, *our*—weddings." She stood and walked across the room, running her fingers along a row of binders before taking one down and bringing it over. She flipped to a full-length picture of another bride and held it in front of Sophie. "She wants one of Jovi's dresses and left it up to me to choose what I think is best. Says she has no idea what to buy anyway and I'd know better."

Sophie studied the woman's figure. Average height, a bit

hippy. "A-line, for sure." She picked up a catalog of Jovi's latest designs that she'd gone through earlier and flipped to the page she had studied when researching dresses for Ty. This bride needed something to accentuate her waist and disguise her hips. "Pull dresses like this one." She pointed. The dress had a wide, flowing skirt with flower embellishments along the bottom, a pretty scoop neckline, and a ruched, gray ribbon at the waist. Perfect.

June glanced back and forth. "You really are amazing at this, Soph. If you keep it up, this won't be the last wedding I put you in charge of." She scooted Sophie out of her chair and sat down.

Sophie folded her arms with satisfaction. Partner at June Pope Weddings before she turned thirty? That sounded very nice, and if Sophie could pull off a spectacular wedding for Rocket Rogers and his bride, June couldn't say no. That meant not letting Ty choose the wrong dress. Sophie was good at this, and she meant for it to stay that way.

chapter eight

AS DAVID WALKED up the sidewalk to his house, he ripped out a page of his Organic Chemistry notebook and crumpled it. He'd taken the final for that class, and his notes revealed he'd bombed one of the major essays.

When he opened the door to the house, the murmur of voices he'd heard through the screen door quieted, and Ty and Anthony looked up at him guiltily from the kitchen table.

He dropped his backpack on the couch and walked straight to the fridge. "I'm not sure if you two know this, but the abrupt stop to your conversation when I walked in gave you away. You're talking about me." He grabbed leftover soup Anthony's mom had sent home with them on Sunday and took a seat at the table, looking from Anthony to Ty and back again. "What's up?"

"It's about this thing with Sophie," Ty started.

David groaned to himself and yanked open the microwave door. "What about her?"

"Well, Anthony wants us to help things along—"

"Smooth, babe."

"What? We've been setting him up for months. It's not like our interest in his love life is new." She smirked.

"True." David punched in numbers to warm up the soup and stared at his friends. "I'm guessing Ty disagrees with setting me up with Sophie—not that I need your help or anything with her."

"Sophie is … deeper than we've given her credit for." Anthony didn't look at Ty when he spoke, a clear sign she disagreed with him.

David turned to Ty. "And you? You don't think so?"

She shook her head and reddened. "It's not that. Sure, she's not my best friend, but Anthony's right. She's done some surprising things the past few weeks. She … she isn't your type. She'd take upkeep. I may not know a lot about fashion and stuff, but I'm pretty sure she lives for it. And she doesn't care all that much about football or a lot of other things that you do care about. I don't think you should get in too deep and be disappointed when things don't work out between you guys because you're too different."

"There's nothing to worry about," David said. "Sophie's not the type of woman I'm going to marry." She'd pulled away from him the minute Anthony had showed up at the party, and even though she'd still brought the cakes for him, she hadn't brought them *just* for him. "Let's talk about something else." He pulled his soup from the microwave. When he turned back to the table to sit down, Ty was watching him, but she averted her eyes and gathered up her and Anthony's lunch dishes.

"Have you talked to Katie lately?" she asked.

He groaned. Out loud this time. "Let's skip the subject of girls."

"What was that phone call about the other night?" Anthony jumped in, moving to help Ty with the dishes. "You never did say." Another topic David would rather avoid. Anthony had always whined about how long baseball games took and claimed the action-packed moments happened few and far between. He'd attended all of David's games in high school out of loyalty but made sure David knew how much he hated it. They'd had this conversation four years ago, and David doubted anything had changed.

"It was that Braves scout, Clint Parry. Offering me a job again."

Anthony chuckled. "Guy can't take no for an answer, can he?"

"I don't know. Maybe there's a reason he keeps calling back."

Might as well broach the subject now. The NFL draft was coming up quicker than David cared for. Plus, spring training had already started for baseball, and if that's what David wanted, the sooner he got to Georgia to join the team, the better for his career. He needed to make a decision, and whether David liked it or not, Anthony was part of it. He was David's best friend and biggest supporter. Every major decision David had made in his life had been with Anthony's help.

Anthony stopped drying a plate and looked up at David. "So you're considering it seriously? What about football?"

David looked down into his soup. "Let's be honest about it. I'm no hotshot like you. Without you at BYU, I wouldn't have gotten noticed in the first place. You don't expect that we're going to go to the same NFL team, do you? Play together again?"

"No." Anthony resumed drying. "But you're a good receiver, whether I'm the one that got you noticed or not."

"Maybe I'll get drafted by a team, maybe I won't. Then what?"

Anthony smirked. "Baseball?"

David laughed. "You're not helping. That's how you've always felt about it."

"But seriously, Beast, most boring game ever. Thought I was going to die watching all those games of yours. And now you want me to watch you for fifteen more years?"

Ty elbowed him. "Be nice."

"You don't like it either, Ty."

Instead of answering, she picked up another dish to wash.

"This is your fault, introducing him to that softball girl—"

"Katie."

"Whatever. I don't know the names of any girls but you."

"Awwww." She stood on her tiptoes and pecked his chin, which was all she could reach.

David dumped his empty soup bowl into the sink to wash later, grabbed his backpack, and headed to his room. Anthony had Ty to distract him from giving out any more useless advice anyway. And watching them had him picturing moments like that for himself—moments with Sophie that hadn't happened yet, as badly as he wanted them to.

David could use a couple hours to blow off some steam. Playing catch had always calmed him, but Anthony wouldn't stoop to throwing a baseball around with him, and David didn't want to just toss a football. The answer popped into his head.

Jay.

Maybe if David showed up at his apartment, he could talk Jay into it. David dug out his mitt and ball from the back of his closet and left the house without Anthony and Ty noticing.

Jay's car was in the parking lot, so David hustled up to the apartment and knocked. Jay answered, his shoulders sagging when he saw David. "Beast. Seriously?"

"I need to play some baseball. You know how Rocket is about that. Oblige me?" He held out the ball.

"Not today." Jay backed behind the door.

David pushed forward, stepping inside before Jay could shut him out. He kept his eyes on Jay, not scrutinizing the mess in the apartment or the beer cans and other party paraphernalia confirming what he already suspected about Jay's reasons for quitting baseball and foregoing a mission.

"So, what's up with you quitting baseball?" David asked.

"I don't want to go over this. I mean, you don't think you're the first one to ask, right?"

"It's either play catch with me or talk about this baseball thing. Your choice." David tugged his mitt on and threw the ball into it a few times. The nice, rhythmic motion calmed him after a couple tosses. Jay's gaze followed the ball with longing. "Come play catch with me, and I'll back off."

Jay glanced up. "You'll back off?"

"For now. Grab your mitt."

Shaking his head, Jay headed down the hall, coming back a few minutes later with a UVU baseball hat and his mitt. He followed David out to a patch of grass that ran between the parking lot of the complex and the street.

David threw first. "So you remember that scout who called me in high school?"

A grin stretched across Jay's face as he caught it. Because they were talking about David instead of him? Or because of the satisfying *thud* of the baseball into his mitt? "Yeah."

"Called me again. Thinks I should play baseball again instead of going to the NFL." David took a few steps back to really throw one at Jay.

"I agree. If you're still good enough."

David wished it were that simple. They threw back and forth in silence for a few minutes, each competing with the other for how hard they could throw it.

"I could be," David said. *Thwack.* He reached in his mitt and threw up a pop fly.

Jay caught it without looking. David shook his head at the arrogant smirk on Jay's face.

"What are you wasting that talent for?" David asked.

Jay tossed the ball in his hands a couple times, avoiding David's gaze now. "You said we didn't have to talk if we played catch."

David drew his hands up in surrender. "Sorry."

"You were saying...?" Jay threw a hard one. "How you might still be good enough to play ball?"

"With some practice." David flung the ball back.

Jay caught it behind his back. He raised his eyebrows, probably waiting for David to make another comment. When David waved him off, feigning indifference, Jay's smile flashed across his face, along with relief.

"Sounds like something you should consider," he said.

"Yeah. Maybe." David widened his mitt, preparing for Jay's throw. He'd take what he could get, and maybe, eventually, Jay would open up.

Sophie needed to ignore the buzz her phone had made. In her pocket. Under her gown. In the middle of the graduation ceremony. But when it buzzed again, she couldn't help brainstorming ways to get it out. The speaker ... wasn't that exciting.

She pulled her arm out of the sleeve of the massive polyester robe without any trouble, ignoring the glower from the guy on her right. She slipped her phone out and then maneuvered her arm back out, resting the phone next to her leg. A text from David.

Of course.

DAVID

What are you doing after graduation?

She bit back a snicker, facing the speaker with her best interested expression and head tilt while tapping out her answer without looking at her phone.

SOPHIE

Seriously. Right now?

Just in case the phone buzzed against the hard-as-a-rock chair she'd sat in for the past six hours—she figured—she flipped it to silent, waiting for the answer by flicking her gaze between the speaker and the phone. (But definitely not toward the guy next to her, who was either checking her out or reproving her, considering how long his stare had burned into her.)

DAVID

No. Not right now. Didn't yup read the text? After. After.

SOPHIE

Yup?

DAVID

Typing without looking. Cut me some slack.

SOPHIE

Never.

DAVID

Of course. So, you busty or what?

Sophie had to stuff her fingers into her mouth to stop a snort of laughter.

SOPHIE

Umm. Don't even know what to come back
with on that one.

DAVID

Any chance we can pretend like that didn't
happen?

SOPHIE

No way.

Sophie scanned the crowd, fighting amusement in case it wasn't appropriate at this juncture in the speech. She didn't spot any tears anywhere. At least that she could see. She hadn't dared glance to her right. In any case, David's next message took a lot longer.

DAVID

Are you avoiding answering whether you're
BUSY or not?

He must have taken his time typing that one to keep from making embarrassing typos.

SOPHIE

Not at all. Thinking hard about my perception
of myself and trying to come up with an answer
for the question before that.

DAVID

Ha. Ha.

SOPHIE

My parents and I are going out to dinner.

DAVID

Chef 's Table?

She started when she read his guess.

SOPHIE

That's just creepy.

DAVID

I know you better than you think.

She hadn't come up with a reply to that before another text
message arrived.

DAVID

Live dangerously and come to a picnic at
Anthony's with us. It's not Chef 's Table, but
way more fun. Promise.

Sophie couldn't argue with that. Chef's Table would be her
and her parents. They got along great, but hanging out with
David sounded a lot more fun. How could she say no?

SOPHIE

Let me check with my mom.

Forgetting she still sat in the Marriott Center, not listening
to a general authority giving the commencement speech, she
opened a new message for her mom.

SOPHIE

What do you say to forgetting about Chef 's Table and picnicking with David's and Anthony's families?

Her mom's answer came back quickly.

MOM

If I thought you could see me glaring, I would have kept my answer to that. Quit texting and listen.

Sophie searched the crowd more intently, wishing she *could* see her mom's face. She tapped out one more message for David.

SOPHIE

My answer will have to wait. Mom told me to quit texting during the speech.

Then she obediently sat on her phone.

The Popes went home long enough to change into more picnic-appropriate clothing and pick up some croissants and chicken salad, their contribution to the lunch taking place in the Rogers' back-yard. When they arrived, Sophie's dad got stopped by a tall, older man that she guessed was Anthony's dad and two guys who looked like David, one with a two-year-old girl on his shoulders. David broke away from the group to greet Sophie. She wished she imag-ined his fleeting glance at her short shorts and the disapproval that briefly followed. It was like Donavan all over again, and that wasn't a welcome feeling. She brushed her fingers over the shorts, disap-pointed he didn't like them. Creating an outfit was her art. Ally teased her for spending twenty or thirty minutes changing time after time to get it perfect, but it was her talent. Like a painter or a sculptor. Did it mean less because she did it with clothes? In any case, she hadn't received her endowment yet, so why did it matter so much if her shorts were a little too short? Why did David have to judge her for it? He wasn't her dad or her bishop or anything.

But her stomach twisted anyway at the thought of David looking at her with the same contempt Donavan had when her clothes weren't quite up to his liking. Somehow, though, it meant more coming from David, and she wondered why. He wasn't blunt or cutting the way Donavan had been. And David hadn't actually *said* anything about her clothes, just looked at her with disappointment and a sad look she didn't quite understand.

Eager to change the unspoken topic to something else, she gestured toward the group they'd left behind as they headed toward the picnic tables lined up next to each other and already filled with food. "Brothers?" she asked, pointing to the two look-alikes.

"Yeah. Older brothers. That's Isaac with his daughter Ruthie —he's the oldest—and the other one is Daniel. Their wives and kids are around here somewhere." David scanned the group in the yard, but before he could point them out, he and Sophie reached the food table. Sophie forgot about introductions as she admired a dark-haired woman with an awesome pixie cut that fit her heart-shaped face. The long bangs fell across her forehead in an effortless way Sophie would kill for. The woman wore a loose white shirt with navy-blue stripes—a great shirt, especially with the knee-length blue shorts she wore, but wrong for her wide-shouldered frame. Still, Sophie loved the outfit, and the haircut made up for it anyway. The woman held out her hands for the massive bowl of chicken salad June had.

"You didn't have to bring anything, considering how last-minute David waited to invite you." The glare the woman gave David made Sophie sure this was his mom.

"You're actually saving me," June said, nudging Sophie to hand over the croissants. "I tried to tell this bride's mom not to order twenty pounds of chicken salad for the luncheon."

David's mom's eyebrows shot up. "Twenty pounds? Good heavens. Who did she think was coming? The football team?" She whirled on Ty's mom, who stood beside her at the table. "How much did you get, Kim?"

Kim shared a look with June. "Twenty pounds," June said, managing to keep a straight face. "But she *is* expecting most of the football team, and we're planning on serving it at the reception too."

While reaching for a cracker with one hand, David's mom shoved out her other. "Forgive me, I should've introduced myself right off. I'm David's mom, Debbie."

"June Pope. Thank you for inviting us. I'm sure Sophie was dreading our boring lunch plans."

Sophie nudged her mom. "No, I wasn't, but I appreciate the invitation too."

"Welcome to the zoo, Sophie." Debbie scooped up chicken salad with the cracker she'd grabbed. She popped it into her mouth. "Holy moly, June!" Debbie cried before she even finished chewing. "Where did you get this? Kim, try this. Now."

Sophie wanted to dissolve into laughter. She loved Debbie immediately. It was no surprise where David got his boisterous personality.

"I don't know how much catering you do"—June chuckled when both Debbie and Kim shook their heads at the same time —"but Liz Allen is superb. We use her whenever we can. If you think this chicken salad is good, you should try her Potato and Corn Chowder."

The other two women sighed with pleasure and scooped up more chicken salad with their crackers.

"Well, at first I thought David asking you to come had something to do with Sophie, but now I see it was all about food." Debbie eyed her son.

"I was hoping they'd show up with cake, to be honest," David said. "That's what Soph normally brings when she comes to my house. She also knows about this other place, a wedding bakery ... you'd never want to leave, Mom. Guarantee it."

Debbie swallowed another bite. "Looks like you people are definitely worth knowing if you've got good food connections."

Sophie leaned toward David again. "Yeah. She's totally your mom."

"Crazy, right?"

"Right."

"Come on, let's blow this popsicle stand before she starts talking about the serious stuff—like ice cream." David put his arm around Sophie's shoulder—a friend move if she ever saw one —and guided her toward some lawn chairs before falling into one.

Sophie settled into the one next to his and took her time surveying the crowd in Anthony's parents' backyard. She found one possibility for David's younger brothers.

"So, you said you had four brothers. I only see three here, unless one of them doesn't look anything like you." She considered a tall boy playing keep-away with Anthony and a group of little boys and one who looked like he might be a deacon. Tossing around a football, of course.

David pointed at the boy Sophie had guessed was one of David's younger brothers. "There's Jonah. My other brother, Noah, is on a mission."

"Daniel, Isaac, David, Noah, Jonah ... I'm sensing a pattern here."

"Really? Like what?" he asked.

Sophie couldn't help the laughter that broke out of her at his faux-innocent expression. How did he do that? She needed to watch it. Her controlled persona slipped with him. But she liked it. David had always had a great sense of humor, and like Anthony, he knew how to flirt with and charm girls, but she'd kept her romantic distance because of his relationship with Anthony. Now that felt like wasted time.

"I bet your mom could raise five more boys and still be

sane. She's awesome." Sophie gazed in that direction again. Debbie was locked in an animated discussion with Kim and June.

"She really is," David said.

Sophie went back to surveying the yard. She found a few possibilities for David's sisters-in-law. She nodded toward one, sitting on the deck with Ty, and loved the floppy straw hat the woman wore with a pair of large, black sunglasses. "Is that one of your sisters-in-law?" Sophie asked.

"No. That's Nikki, Anthony's sister. But since we all grew up together, she's like a sister to me too." He averted his eyes and tapped the arm of his lawn chair.

Sophie sat back, stunned. Anthony had never said a word about having a sister. Not even in passing. As she contemplated it, Debbie left Kim and June at the table and headed toward Ty and Nikki. Ty hopped up when she came over, and Debbie took her chair. Ty joined the keep-away game in the grass. Pretty soon Jonah had joined as well, and soon a football game had started. Sophie giggled when the littlest boy stood in front of Anthony, ready to hike the ball.

"Most adorable center I've ever seen," she said to David. "Don't tell Sean."

"We need a good center now that Sean's graduating. Eli will make a great replacement. That's Nikki's youngest." He stood up. "You coming to play?" His gaze ran over her outfit, which wasn't the best for football playing, even though she'd changed after graduation.

She kicked off the pale blue heels she wore and pushed up the sleeves of her slouchy shirt. "Of course."

It was a good thing the Rogerses had a huge backyard. By the time David and Sophie made it over to play, David's older brothers and even Sophie's dad had joined the game. They split into teams, Sophie and David being the first on one side and Ty and Anthony on the other.

"Not fair," David said. "No offense, Soph, but Ty's like a bajillion times better than you."

"Wow. Thanks." She shoved him.

"No problem." He dropped an arm over her shoulders. He hadn't offended her. She didn't care enough about football—or any sport—to get upset about it. She had her own strengths. She played those up. "Anyway, we get Walsh then." He was a star player at his high school, so he might make up some of the talent difference.

"You're going to regret that when I take Harly," Anthony said. Harly, Ty's seven-year-old brother, jumped and pumped both fists into the air.

Sophie leaned over to David. "I've always had a preference for frilly little girls," she said under her breath. "But all the adorable little boys here are making me rethink that position."

David ignored the way his neck tingled when a breeze blew part of her hair toward him. The way she grabbed up her long, brown hair and started twisting it around on top of her head mesmerized him for a minute. Better to gawk at her hair—it looked shiny and soft, and he wanted to bury his face or maybe even his hands in it—than to find his eyes drawn to her bare shoulder, where her shirt had shifted to reveal the strap of a pink tank top and skin. He looked away to be safe, cleared his throat, and tried to come up with something to say. Harly. She'd said something about Harly.

"Harly is perhaps the coolest kid I know. We will regret not having him." David rolled the football around in his hands, trying to concentrate on how to split the teams up. By not looking over at Sophie again, he managed to focus and choose a decent team. They ended up with Nikki's oldest son, four-year-old Porter; David's brother, Isaac; and Sophie's dad.

Sophie was horrendous, and the best part was that she tried anyway. He pictured her playing football like a girly-girl, closing her eyes when she tried to catch or being scared of getting into the pile. But the first catch he threw to her, which she promptly dropped, she dove right on top of, faking surprise when Eli came up with it a few seconds later.

He'd come to think of Sophie as synonymous with high-maintenance. High heels. Jewelry. Never dirty. Worried about broken nails. Not a woman who pretended to dive after an almost-two-year-old when he scored a touchdown for the other team. She did scowl at the lengthy grass stain on her gray shorts —as lengthy as it could be considering the lack of length to the shorts. But a second later the frown disappeared.

David looked over at Ty, wondering what she would think. She hefted Eli into her arms and cheered with him, but she must have felt David's stare. When she met his gaze she shrugged, but he didn't get the "what-do-ya-know" vibe from it. He blew out a sigh. He didn't need Ty or Anthony or anybody's permission to date Sophie, if it ever came to that.

"She's getting married soon, so I'd say your chance with her has passed." Sophie's voice snapped David's attention to where she stood in front of him.

"Believe me, I tried."

Wrong thing to say. Sophie's eyebrows crinkled before she shifted the expression from hurt to indifference. The connotations of that simple sentence hit him ten seconds too late. Already Anthony had passed over Sophie for Ty, and now David too? Especially when he was trying to show her how real guys treated girls? Fail.

He wasn't quite sure how to do damage control. He hooked an arm around her neck, pulling her into a mock headlock. "Nice fumble, by the way."

"Sorry, not as good at football as Ty either."

So. Not working. He tried to keep up with the joking. "Or Harly for that matter, but that's not surprising. Maybe if you put your shoes back on you can stab a few people in the shins. That would help." He let her go so he could hold her by the shoulders in front of him and chase away the disappointment he'd caused.

"Anyone in particular you'd like me to take out first?" The edge hadn't left her voice yet, but at least she was playing along.

"I'd say Anthony, but maybe we should focus on his receivers first and force him to run."

She arched her eyebrows. "That's your play call? I thought Anthony was pretty good at running."

"Play call?" He inched closer. "Nice football terminology there, Pope. I think I've underestimated you."

She gave him a small smile. "You better believe you have." Her shoulders relaxed.

Now how did he swoop in and finish this off? "But seriously? I'd take you over Harly any day. He's never brought me cake in his life."

She laughed, though not with as much giggle as some of her other laughs had sometimes. "Any more talk about my serious lack of football skills, and I may tell Genevieve not to let you into her bakery ever again."

"You are pure evil."

She jabbed her finger in his chest and then fingered his shirt for a second before she dropped it. "And don't forget it." She bumped him with her shoulder as she went by.

David absently rubbed at the spot where her fingers had lingered, like that was all it took to forget the zing she made go through him every time she touched him. Yes. Pure evil. And a total pro.

chapter nine

AFTER PLAYING catch with Jay for a couple hours on Tuesday, David needed to play some baseball and figure out if he even had a chance of being good at center field again. Then he could start figuring out his football-baseball situation. David got up the courage to call the BYU baseball coach and ask to crash their practice. But knowing that he needed to really get his hand in a mitt and swing a bat didn't make walking into his first baseball practice in a few years any easier.

The coach met him in the hallway outside the locker room, his hand stuck out. "David Savage. This is quite a surprise. Didn't expect to see you again after you turned me down six years ago."

David pumped his hand with a chuckle. "To be honest, I didn't expect it myself, but here I am."

"Go ahead and get changed in the locker room. You chose a good day to come. I've got some relay throwing drills and cut-offs with runners to do. That should tell you how well your arm has held up with all the catching you've been doing instead of throwing." He slapped David on the shoulder and walked toward his office. "See you out on the field."

David rolled his right shoulder back. He'd tossed footballs in the last few years, but not enough to stay competitive at center field. He pushed the locker room door open, hoping he didn't make a fool of himself out there on the field.

By the time he finished changing and walked out with a couple of the guys, his anxiety had eased—a little. He'd played with and against some of them in high school. Their joking with him about choosing the wrong sport kept things light as they all stretched and warmed up. At least David could say he'd kept in shape. And maybe that game of catch with Jay had helped too, even if he hadn't talked Jay into another round since then. David had texted him when he hadn't come to the graduation picnic, but Jay had blown him off, saying that since Noah wasn't there, he didn't need to show. David would have to keep trying, for his own sake and Jay's.

When the team started the relay drills, the coach had the regular center fielder go first, probably to remind David how to play the game. As he stepped up to take the player's place a few minutes later, he shook out his arms and hoped for the best.

He caught the ball one of the assistant coaches tossed him and eyed the second baseman, who stood off his base and on the grass, ready to catch David's throw and relay it to home base. Taking a deep breath, David wound up and threw as hard as he could, hoping he made it far enough not to look like a sissy.

It ended up way over the second baseman's head, but David laughed with relief. At least he hadn't underthrown it. Things went better from there. The rest of the tension melted away. He could at least throw it as far as ever. Sure, he was rusty, but by the time they'd run through a few more drills and gotten in some batting practice, he knew with more work he could compete in baseball again. No straight shot to a major league team, but a good chance of doing something—if he wanted to. Did he?

"Not bad, Savage, not bad." The coach patted him on the shoulder as the rest of the team headed for the showers.

"Thanks." David ran his fingers along the laces of his mitt and made a decision. He still had a lot of thinking to do before he committed to baseball, but he needed to know if he should give it a shot. "Mind if I come to a few practices? Stay loose and in shape so I don't embarrass myself." He kept his wording vague. If he gave away that he still thought about playing in the NFL, the coach might not be so willing to help him out.

"No problem. We'd be glad to have you. See you Monday then." The coach gave him another shoulder pat and trotted down the hall toward his office.

"See you Monday," David said to himself and grinned.

David had never pictured Anthony as the type of guy to have one of those fancy, black-tie engagement parties he'd seen in the few chick-flick movies he'd been forced to watch. But June Pope Weddings put it in as part of the package Sophie had gotten for them, and, as best man, David was required to attend. His shoulder was stiff from practice earlier that day, and he almost tried to wiggle out of going. Except—Sophie would be there. It wouldn't hurt to put in some quality time with her.

And he didn't regret that decision when he walked in and saw Sophie directing things in her fancy pink dress, except he couldn't get near her most of the night. She escorted Ty and Anthony here and there. Directed guests and staff alike. Kept the happy couple on a schedule. Never once noticed him. Could she still be mad about what he'd said about Ty at the picnic? Sophie had continued to flirt with him the rest of the night, but he never knew with girls. He never knew with Sophie especially.

Maybe Ty was right about her. Sophie had a mind of her own and got her way when she wanted to. He'd watched her handle Anthony with finesse, and in the two years he'd known her, she'd played everything right with Anthony. She hadn't let on that their off-and-on relationship bothered her, and she'd stuck around as a friend when they were off—and more when he showed interest in dating her again. She'd followed a strategy to patiently reel him in. As luck would have it, she wasn't the woman for Anthony.

David had wanted someone more like Ty. Someone who could wear a pair of sweats and go out with him to McDonalds. He recalled what Ty had said about Sophie's taste in expensive clothes. He didn't know much about that, but tonight, Sophie definitely looked expensive. Could Sophie pull off McDonalds runs and sweats? Would she even want to? She'd played football. It was a start.

"To heck with Ty and her pessimism." He straightened his tie, checked himself out in the reflection of a nearby window, and strode toward Sophie.

"Busy?" he asked, cutting into her conversation with a guest he didn't recognize. Ty's side? Maybe. But Sophie had invited some important people—proof that she was at least a little right when she'd said she could do Anthony's career good.

Sophie glanced at him and stumbled over a couple words. The guests shared a look with each other, and David watched—with pleasure—as red crept into Sophie's cheeks. So, at least he could unsettle her and not just the other way around.

"Didn't you say you wanted to dance, dear?" The man held his arm out to his wife.

She took it, a twinkle lighting her eyes as she watched David and Sophie. "I would love to."

After they'd walked away, Sophie put her hands on her hips. "Do you know who that was?"

"Not a clue, but they're right. We should dance too."

"I don't have time for that."

"If I take you outside, no one will be able to find you. Then you'll have time to dance." He threaded his fingers through hers and dragged her toward some open French doors. She resisted at first and shifted away from him, tensing when he stopped on the edge of the light coming from inside. He'd come to this party to see her. He would dance with her. He wrapped an arm around her waist, lightly massaging away the tension in her back.

"What are you doing?" she asked, but she let him take her hand and rest it against his chest.

"Dancing with you. Don't you deserve a minute to enjoy all your hard work?" She'd been on her feet all night. He'd know. He'd watched her sashay here and there, looking professional and irresistible at the same time.

The tension in her jaw and expression softened. She relaxed into his arms. "You're telling me that the first thing you noticed tonight was how hard I was working?" she asked.

Checking her out would not do anything for showing her that looks weren't everything, as much as he wanted to do just that. He kept his staring to her face. That's when he noticed her eyes. Her gorgeous, hazel eyes with gold rims.

"Yeah," he answered two minutes too late.

She laughed and leaned closer. That's when he noticed her lips. Those he was pretty familiar with. They'd taken over his mind since that day at the cake shop. Especially the idea of his lips and her lips together.

He cleared his throat and tried to focus. Sophie wasn't the type of woman a guy like him married. He shouldn't lead her on if he didn't intend to take her seriously. That sounded more like Donavan's style. So he shouldn't think so much about her lips. Flirting with her around their families in a game of backyard football was one thing. Dancing this close to her was playing with fire.

"You want to sit down?" he asked, motioning toward a stone bench. "You could probably use a break."

She turned, but didn't increase the distance between them. "That depends." She looked back at him. "Are you going to finish that foot rub?"

"Gladly." Foot rubs were all about appreciation, right? That was always how his mom had insisted he show it. No big deal.

Keeping his hand in hers, because she might run back inside if he didn't, of course, he led her to the bench and sat down. She sat next to him, kicking her heels off before lifting a leg and extending it toward him.

He wrapped his hand around her foot, but this time it wasn't as innocent to him. He noticed she didn't tense like she had the first time. He glanced up at her.

She wore a relaxed expression as she tipped her head toward him. "I don't know many guys willing to give foot rubs like you do. Why'd you keep that secret from me all this time I've known you? Seems unfair to think about how many of these I've missed out on."

He chuckled and stared down at her foot. He'd never noticed how small it was. Not that he routinely noticed girls' feet, but hers were especially girly, her toenails painted pink to match her dress. He swallowed and forced his fingers into action.

"Maybe I should have told you," he said, trying to keep things light and not let the intensity he felt in the moment get the better of him. "Maybe you would've paid more attention to me than Anthony."

She tilted her head in a silent *touché*. "Maybe. How'd you get so good at it? Been sharing this talent with all the other girls you date?"

"Foot rubs are my mom's favorite. She said I gave the best because I was always working out and had big muscles, or something ridiculous like that. Her way of praising me into doing something." He pictured his mom's feet to keep his thoughts off the way Sophie had her legs draped across his lap. Calluses and dry, rough skin covered his mom's feet since she ran around everywhere without shoes or in flip-flops, even in the middle of December. That made Southern California a better fit for her now than American Fork had ever been. But Sophie's weren't like that. No calluses. Soft...

"She must have raised you right, then." Sophie broke into his thoughts. "Of course I knew that from the moment I met her."

"There aren't words to describe how fantastic she is. She's

had five boys to perfect her methods on. I imagine she just has to look at Jonah at this point and he knows what to do."

"The youngest one, right?"

"Right."

"Maybe she just wiggles her toes." Sophie demonstrated.

David laughed and made the mistake of looking up at her again.

She'd bent over her legs, closer to him, her shoulder almost touching his arm. Here he was holding her foot. Her soft, dainty foot with pale pink nails, when he'd rather put his arm around her and—

Before he could stop, he reached one hand toward her face, brushing over her chin first with his knuckle, then his thumb. She held her breath, and David took that as an invitation to shorten the distance between their faces. He ran his finger along her cheek.

He shouldn't kiss her. That would lead her on, wouldn't it? Like Ty had accused, because he wanted a different woman than Sophie.

He swallowed.

What kind of different? He couldn't remember. Something about girls who didn't wear heels all the time. The kind of woman who didn't have to have painted toenails even when no one would see her feet.

Not Sophie.

Except right now, he found her pink toenails endearing, and he thought that after knowing each other for at least two years and hanging out together all the time, that having not come to this moment sooner was a waste of time. Why *not* Sophie? Why not a woman who could call him out for planning a lame birthday party for his best friend and then plan exactly what David wanted to but even better? Why not a woman who knew him like that, even if she came off as high maintenance? He couldn't answer that right now, and that scared him.

"They're probably looking for you in there." But he didn't want to pull away yet.

Her eyebrows pushed down, shrouding her hazel eyes with confusion. "Yeah..." She didn't move either.

Slowly and with a lot of reluctance, he put her feet on the sidewalk and pulled her up, keeping her hand in his. He had to have some consolation, some prize for not giving in and kissing her. He brushed the top of her hand with his thumb while he waited for her to slip her shoes back on.

She contemplated him, questioning. "You only seem capable of rubbing one of my feet at a time."

He forced a hollow laugh. "I have to save something to do later."

"Oh." A shadow of a smile crossed her face, and then she walked with him back inside. David didn't have to catch Ty's disappointed frown to feel like a heel.

Except, was he mad at himself for leading Sophie on and almost kissing her?

Or for not kissing her?

chapter ten

BY THE NEXT MORNING, Sophie still could not figure out what had happened the night before to stop David from kissing her, and more frustratingly, how he'd curled her toes more with anticipation just by an *almost* kiss than any other real kiss had in her life.

David had wanted to kiss her last night. Touching her face like he did. His expression full of expectation. So why hadn't he? He acted interested. Flirting, rubbing her feet, making her dance with him.

Or maybe it was the same old thing: a guy thinking she's hot and dating her for the chance to make out. But maybe David was too much of a gentleman to kiss her if he didn't mean it.

She wished he had anyway. Even if he didn't mean it.

And she liked that he thought enough about her feelings to not do it.

And she wanted to yell and hit things and eat a lot of ice cream. So instead of pounding her pillow, she plodded downstairs and raided the freezer. Luckily for her, Ally kept it pretty well stocked with the good stuff—Ben and Jerry's. Sophie had downed most of the carton of Cheesecake Brownie when Ally walked in.

She froze halfway to the kitchen, shock plain on her face. "What are you doing?"

Sophie scowled. "Eating ice cream. What does it look like?"

"What *happened* last night?" Ally dropped her purse and sat on one of the metal barstools at the counter that separated the kitchen and living room.

Sophie's scowl deepened, and she glared at the half-gone ice cream. At this rate she'd have to replenish the stock soon. "David was *this close*"—she held up two fingers less than an inch apart—"and didn't kiss me. Nothing. Gawked at me all hot and bothered for a few minutes and then told me I needed to get back to the party. This. Close." She walked across the kitchen and leaned over so her lips were inches from Ally's face. "Is there something wrong with them?"

"Well, they are covered in ice cream right now. Maybe you should've done that last night. He wouldn't have been able to resist licking a couple bites of Ben and Jerry's off."

"Ha ha. So funny." Sophie straightened, scraped out a few more bites and devoured them, all while Ally watched in wonder.

"How is it that you don't get ice cream headaches?" Ally asked.

"It's a gift."

The doorbell rang. With one final shake of her head, Ally hurried to answer the door. Sophie finished off the ice cream. "Ugh. I just ate an entire pint of ice cream." Extra miles on the treadmill tonight for sure.

"Does that mean you're too full for dinner?" David's voice asked from the front door.

Gaping, Sophie looked up. Gathering her wits, she dumped the ice cream carton in the trash and licked off the spoon before tossing it toward the sink—and missing. It clattered to the floor.

"Nice." David raised his eyebrows as he entered the kitchen. Then they jumped farther up before he smoothed out his expression.

The fact that David had showed up at her house despite last

night's disastrous non-kissing episode almost cancelled out her disappointment from him not kissing her the night before. But something was going on with him.

"What's wrong?" she asked.

He shrugged, too innocently. "Nothing."

She glared at him, waiting for him to give her a good answer. "Your dress is ... uh ... aren't you cold? Do you need a sweater or ... something?" He forced a smile.

Yeah, there was no mistaking the judgment now. She scrutinized her outfit. Like David and the rest of his roommates, she and Ally had graduated last Thursday, so she didn't need to worry about BYU's dress code anymore. Plus, it'd been hot today, even for spring, so she'd worn one of her favorite, comfortable minidresses, a spaghetti strap, with a pair of soft, bright-pink leggings. Comfort at its hottest.

"You don't like the way I dress?" she asked bluntly. Okay, first the almost-kiss. Now this. She might as well get David to show his true, Donavan-like colors and get the critiquing over with. Then she could rip into him for his judgments, send him packing, and get him out of her head for good.

"Play nice, Soph," Ally said under her breath as she walked past to go upstairs.

"It's nothing, Soph. It doesn't matter what I think. I came to ask you if you wanted to go get something to eat." He rested against the back of the couch, watching her—but keeping his eyes on her face. Except ... every time he talked to her, he made it a point to look into her eyes, which was good, she guessed. But something told her it wasn't because he wanted to gaze longingly into her soul. Was she reading too much into this?

She put her hands on her hips, determined to figure him out right there. "What's wrong with the way I dress?"

He sighed and rolled his eyes to the ceiling before looking back at her again. "Nothing, as long as it makes you feel good. Strong and confident. As long as you feel like you." He shoved his hands in his pockets.

Of course she felt like herself in this dress. She had a million ways to dress it up or down. Plus, there was something David hadn't said.

"There's a 'but' in that sentence." She knew what that "but" was, that he thought she was dressed immodestly. She wanted to hear him say it and have it out right here. Forget that he made her feel all soft and melty inside.

"Sophie ... I just want to know if you want to go get something to eat with me." He pulled out one of his hands and rubbed his chin, not looking at her.

"Spit it out."

"Fine." He met her gaze again. "Wouldn't you rather that a guy liked you because you're smart and a blast to be around rather than having him ogle you all the way through dinner?"

"My right to wear this dress has nothing to do with whether you'll ogle me or not. That's on you," she snapped.

"You're exactly right. Should we go?" He moved toward the door, holding out a hand to her.

Sophie hated that he'd given in so easily when she wanted to argue this point with him. To prove he was just like Donavan and not the good guy. She *knew* he didn't agree with her choices. How could she prove him wrong about it when he agreed too readily?

"I never said yes," she pointed out instead of following.

He dropped his hand. "Are you going to?"

"Are you going to want me to change?" She folded her arms and frowned at him.

He frowned back, but it looked more confused than anything. "No..."

Her fingers itched to slap him for being so ... so ... compliant.

"And you can keep yourself from staring at me long enough to have a conversation with me?"

His go-to, mischievous smile showed up now. "I'll try."

"Okay, let's go," she said. He held his hand back up for her, and she took it.

David didn't say anything as he led her down the sidewalk, and Sophie's thoughts shifted to Donavan again. If she could say one thing about him, it was that he got her love of fashion. He understood the art she saw in it. So, yeah, the perfectionism he'd demanded from her was stupid, but that didn't mean her ability to put together a great outfit was too, did it?

She'd spent the last three years perfecting her style to show off the confident woman she wanted to be. Sophie was smart, but smart girls weren't always noticed. Her beauty got her attention, and she had a knack for making the most of it. She should use that.

David opened the door for her and put his hand on her back to guide her inside. What was going on with them? She wanted him to scoop his arm around her waist like he had at the cake shop and pull her close. But did he just want to stay friends?

She watched him as he slid into the driver's seat. David had such an adorable charm. She'd always liked the way his hair curled up a bit at the ends. It gave him a playful look. And, okay, so the knight in shining armor guarding her virtue bit wasn't half bad either.

"What's all the staring for?" He rested his arm on the console between them. Should she reach up and hold his hand, or would he pull away?

She wanted to slap herself on the forehead. Sophie never worried about how a guy would react to her flirting. She could take them or leave them. Even David.

"Sophie?" His grin said he read her expression perfectly.

"Uh, what?" He'd asked a question. She decided to deflect it by flirting. She laid her hand on his arm. Her instincts urged her to purr something like, "I can't help it." Another part of her started laughing. "Yeah. Okay. I was ogling you. Sometimes being covered up doesn't matter."

David joined in. "My right to be this handsome has nothing to do with whether you'll ogle me or not. That's on you," he said.

She shook her head at him. "Good one." She tapped her

fingers on the console, studying him again. "You don't act like most guys about modesty."

He started the car and pulled away. "Giving a foot rub isn't the only thing my mom taught me to do right," he said. "She taught me to respect girls with my actions *and* my thoughts, no matter what they wore. You can choose what you wear because it's your body. I can choose what I think because this is mine."

"She's a smart lady."

"You'd have to be to keep a step ahead of all those boys, right?" He chuckled.

His words about controlling his thoughts reminded her of a boy in her ward in high school and the way he made his choices about controlling them. "How firm a foundation, ye saints of the Lord," she started singing, and giggling.

"What ... are you doing?" David arched an eyebrow, like he meant to mock her crazy reaction, but laughter shook his words.

"A friend of mine used to sing hymns to keep from thinking impure thoughts."

"My mom had me memorize scriptures," he said and started humming along. They finished off the hymn in breathy vibratos, taking twice as long as it should have since they laughed all the way through.

"So where are we going?" David asked.

"Where are we going?" She looked around. He'd been changing lanes and turning and acting like he knew what he was doing for the last five minutes. "I figured you had somewhere in mind."

"I didn't want to interrupt our moment." He took her hand back in his and squeezed it before letting go. "Where to?"

She considered letting him choose. Then she considered picking something nice, not quite upscale, but maybe out of the way and romantic. But that didn't sound right for a night out with David. How long had it been since she'd had a greasy hamburger? Ages. And he was the perfect guy to eat a greasy hamburger with.

"Red Robin?"

He stopped at the light at University Parkway and 550 West. "You? Red Robin? I doubt it."

"What's that supposed to mean?" She attempted to glare at him sternly.

"That your idea of greasy food is Café Rio."

She did usually make guys take her to nice places, less grease. No kids' meals. "I'm addicted to their bottomless fries."

He crossed the left-turn lane, cutting off another car. "Well, I'm not going to argue. I might even have a coupon in my wallet."

"Classy, Beast. Classy."

He grinned, and it was the sexiest grin she'd ever seen.

David would have never thought in a million years that he'd spend a car ride with Sophie Pope singing every hymn they could think of at the top of their lungs. Or that she'd choose to eat at Red Robin. She made the just-friends thing hard for him. Especially when he watched her eyes dance with laughter as they tried to stay on key while shout-singing "Book of Mormon Stories." Even though she challenged him at every turn, hanging out with a woman had never been easier.

After the waitress left with their orders, Sophie leaned over the table. "So, have you made a decision about football and baseball?"

"Not yet."

"When do you have to know?" She twirled her straw in her lemonade and watched him.

He rubbed his hand over his eyes. When he'd submitted his name to the draft all those months ago, it was the natural thing to do—Anthony had, of course. Why not David? Now his feelings had changed so much. "The NFL draft is in a couple weeks. Before then."

Ranee S. Clark

"Which one do you like more?"

"It's hard to say." So far, he'd been preoccupied with how he and Sophie had only flirted and almost kissed and how not-serious their relationship was—but NFL or baseball meant leaving Provo. Leaving anything he started here.

"No wonder you're clueless." She sat back, still keeping her gaze on him. "Okay, pros of playing football?"

He took a second to wipe his brain of what they'd maybe started. What he wanted to start. He focused on the things he'd gone over in his mind before, hoping that giving it a voice would also bring clarity to his decision. "I've got a pretty good chance of making a team, though it's not a given. Find me a great quarterback, and I'll do great things."

"Like you have with Anthony."

"Yeah."

"Cons?" she asked.

"Not making a team. Making a team and not ever playing except in practice."

"And baseball?"

The waitress came with the towering onion rings they'd ordered as soon as they got there. To his surprise, Sophie had chosen them. He'd expected her to order the spinach dip. Thank heavens she hadn't. He couldn't have choked it down, and after the way the night had started, he didn't want to hurt her feelings again.

"Well?" Sophie prodded when the waitress left.

It'd felt good to throw a baseball again. To swing a bat. Running in a touchdown made his adrenaline pump—but hitting a line drive? A home run? It was one of the hardest things to do in sports, and he could. A couple hours of catch had brought the flicker of his love of baseball back. Practice the day before had fanned it to life. "I love baseball. I've loved it for a while. And maybe there's a chance I'll play great again on my own..." He hadn't meant to add *on my own*.

116

Sophie guessed his meaning, of course. "Out from under Anthony's shadow."

"It's been a good shadow," he insisted. And it had. That first pass he'd caught from Anthony—the way it fell into his hands, how he'd had to take only a couple extra steps, in *seventh* grade no less. They'd known each other so well, it made every play effortless. Every win was more fun than the last, year after year.

"It's not a bad thing to want to show who you are without him. You can still be his best friend and want that. Cons?"

"I haven't played seriously in almost five years. I could end up playing the next ten years on a triple-A team, hoping to move up. When would I know to give up and get a real job?"

"That could happen in football too," she pointed out.

"Way to make it easier." He chuckled.

"I say baseball."

"Just like that?"

"You smiled more when you talked about it."

She'd noticed that? She had paid pretty close attention to him since they'd gotten in the car. Here they sat, eating greasy onion rings together, something he hadn't thought possible with Sophie, something he figured her high heels, expensive clothes, and driven attitude made her too high-strung to enjoy. He'd started keeping a tally in his head of all the un-Sophie things she'd done around him. Playing football with kids—and enjoying it. Choosing Red Robin. Ordering something besides salad. Did that mean a quiet evening on the couch with a movie and some cuddling wasn't such a far-fetched idea either?

"Since I chose football, I've planned on doing that as long as I could. It feels almost crazy to consider doing anything else," he said.

She grabbed an onion ring and dipped it in enough ranch to choke a horse. "Not that crazy."

"The way you eat onion rings is quite possibly the most attractive thing about you."

He wanted to take it back as soon as he said it. It wasn't a very flattering comment, and Sophie thrived on other people's approval. Instead she licked some ranch off her fingers, which threw David for another loop. She had a way of upending him like that.

"I haven't had onion rings in a long time. I'm enjoying this."

"Me too."

"'Because it reminds you of growing up with four brothers?"

"You're a lot prettier than my brothers."

She dragged another onion ring through the ranch. "I dress better too."

"Yeah, they would all look horrible in that dress." He paused and took the last onion ring before Sophie could. "Well, Jonah's still kind of skinny. Maybe he could pull it off."

She swallowed her onion ring and grabbed the side David hadn't eaten. "You're saying I pull it off?"

"I never said you didn't. It's just ... distracting." With a half-smile he started humming "How Firm a Foundation" again. The waitress who brought their food a few seconds later eyed him, but Sophie laughed.

"So, the guy who sang all the hymns," David asked when the waitress left. "Did you date him?"

"Nah. He didn't go for girls like me."

"Girls like you?" David hefted his guacamole bacon burger. "Confident, gorgeous girls?"

Her eyes lit up. "Girls who dress like me. Someone walking on the edge. We went out on a date once. He told me in the gentlest way possible that I wasn't his type. He didn't want a girl-friend before his mission, and I was too forward."

"Too forward?" David didn't think there was such a thing. A woman who didn't force him to play games and guess about her? "Are you still too forward?"

"Probably. Doesn't matter. He got married, like within days of getting home, I think." She chuckled. "To a nice girl who probably deserved him."

Deserved him? As in she didn't? "So you went off and dated

someone who deserved you? Like Donavan?" He scowled. The hymn-singing guy, even though he hadn't meant to, had contributed to Sophie's self-esteem issues more than she gave him credit for.

"Donavan is the type of guy who notices girls like me." She focused her concentration on her fries.

"It's hard not to notice you, Sophie. You command a room, and you know that. Every guy notices you."

She stirred one of her fries around in the fry sauce. "Not all of them ask me out. Not the nice ones, like you."

"And what is this?" He gestured to the table full of food that he intended to pay for.

"We're friends, like we have been for the past two years." She sat back and studied him. "This isn't the first time we've been out to eat together." She shrugged at him.

"It's the first time it's been just the two of us."

"Are you calling this a date then?" she asked.

Dare he hope that the slight pink rising in her cheeks meant that she wanted it to be a date? "I asked you out to eat food. Yes, I call that a date. So tell me about your family. Brothers? Sisters?"

"Just me. I was about all my mom could handle. Or so she says."

"What does your dad do?"

"He's a lawyer."

David couldn't help laughing at that. She'd inherited some arguing skills. Maybe her stubbornness. Her get-it attitude. But that could come from her mom too. You didn't become a successful businesswoman by sitting back.

"Yeah. Yeah. I'm a lot like him."

"So are you pre-law?" It surprised David that after knowing her for so long he didn't know her major. Considering the number of times they'd hung out together, shouldn't that have come up in conversation sometime? What kind of friend to her was he these past few years if he didn't even know that?

"Nope. Public relations."

"What are you going to do with that?"

"Produce my own reality TV show." She dipped a couple french fries in her quickly diminishing ranch. "Or partner at June Pope Weddings. Or start my own consulting business. Or ..." She took a bite of the french fry and let the sentence hang while she finished. "The wife of an NFL player."

Despite knowing which future NFL player she meant, David didn't miss a beat. "Talking about marrying me on the first date? Really, Sophie? You're better than that."

She ate another fry. "I'm losing my touch."

"Too full from that ice cream for a challenge?" he asked. "What?"

"Whoever refills their fries the least amount of times pays?"

"You're on."

When she got home that night, Sophie stood in front of her closet and scrutinized her clothes, thinking about how David said they distracted him. She'd always had a specific date style, different from what she'd worn every day on campus. Usually skirts or dresses—sure, short ones—but she liked lace and ruffles and dressing up. Always high heels. Accessories. Her favorite part of a date, in most cases, was getting ready: pulling out a starting piece, like a shirt in her favorite color, a new skirt, or great shoes, and pairing all the right things with it. She'd focused so much on that, maybe she hadn't seen herself objectively.

A shimmery tank dress stuck out between some other dresses, and she reached in and pulled it out. The straps were wide—kind of. And it hit her above her knee, but not in a scandalous way. Yeah, so it wasn't exactly modest, but she didn't think it was too bad. She'd worn it the night Anthony kissed her for the first time. She used to remember that night with excitement and fond nostalgia, but now she frowned. They'd gone to a nice restaurant, and Anthony had sat *right* next to her all night.

He'd had an arm around her, hugging her close or putting his hand on her knee the whole time. He'd watched her, appreciative. And his gaze had swept over her more than a few times. Her heart had fluttered then, to have him admire her like that. He'd done it right before he kissed her, leaning in and murmuring something about not being able to resist, considering the way she looked.

That had happened less than twenty minutes into the date, and they didn't talk much that night either. Or on any of their dates, for that matter. Light stuff, maybe. About an upcoming game or homework they might have. Not about his sister—or any of his family. Not like she had with David tonight. Not about their futures, separately or together. After a couple weeks of dates, he would take out another woman. They would break up, or things would just slide into casual dating, and she didn't let it bother her. He had a reputation for going on a few dates with girls then cutting them loose. Before Ty, he'd always come back to her. If anything, she'd lasted a lot longer than the rest of them did.

She'd kept dressing to get his attention—to *keep* his attention or to wrest it away from some new woman. It had been a successful tactic so far. Besides, she'd told herself, he'd settle down eventually. And he had. Just not with Sophie. Instead, he settled down with a woman who threw a cardigan on and called it dressy.

So how had Ty kept his attention? Was David on to something? Maybe the fact that Anthony and Ty had fewer "distractions" in their relationship led to what they had now. What had Anthony said? That Ty knew the real Anthony Rogers. And Ty probably felt the same way about him.

Sophie put the dress away and contemplated the closet a while longer. She had plenty of clothes to cover up more—she'd gone to BYU for four years and followed the honor code. New outfit possibilities bloomed in her mind, her excitement growing with each one.

She liked David. The idea of having a relationship with him like Anthony and Ty's appealed to her. And as she reached for more clothes, she considered the possibility that maybe she didn't need clothes to be noticed. Not the way she thought she did.

Sophie Pope had always liked facing a challenge and smashing it to pieces. This one would be no different.

chapter eleven

DAVID WIPED the sweat from his forehead and rolled onto his back in the grass. "No more weeds. Not even Nikki could find weeds." He tipped his head to one side to eye Anthony, still bent over the flowerbed and running his fingers along the dirt. "What's your sister got on you that she talked you into weeding her and your mom's flowerbeds?"

"I offered to do it so she'd have less to worry about."

"How's she doing with everything, going back to church and all that?" David asked.

Anthony sat down and sighed. "Good, considering. Her anxiety is worse than normal, but you know, she has OCD, and she just started associating with about 150 extra people a week."

David chuckled. He'd spent more than a few lunch hours in high school sitting at a table with Nikki and Anthony and keeping too many people from sitting down near them. "She came to the graduation picnic, so that's something. It was good to have her around again."

"Yeah. Mom's been helping her choose which meetings to go to for now. Writing it down. Doing stuff to help her feel a lot more in control of the situation." Anthony grinned. "Whatever it takes to get her there makes me happy."

"Exactly."

"So are you still thinking about choosing baseball?" Anthony asked.

David shook his head. "It wouldn't be the end of the world if I did."

"Close enough." Anthony laughed. "You've only got two and a half more weeks."

"I know, I know." David turned to the sky and closed his eyes. "Every time I think I've decided one way or the other, I come up with something I'd miss. Is this what that scripture means about a 'stupor of thought'?"

"Probably. Football it is."

"Ha. Except I have a stupor of thought whenever I try to choose. Football *and* baseball," David said. Unless he went with Sophie's advice to choose baseball because he looked happier.

Anthony's phone dinged, distracting him. The excitement in his face told David Ty had texted him. David pulled out his own phone, wishing Sophie had texted him just because. What was going on with them? More than friends? How could he move it to the next level and still keep his promise to treat her like a real friend?

"What's up?" David asked to annoy Anthony.

"Walsh says it's slow at the aquatic center over at the Rec Center today, and his manager says he can get us in for cheap. Ty wants to know if we want to go."

"That sounds perfect right about now." David checked his watch. He had a few hours before baseball practice. "Just us three?" David rubbed some of the sweat from his face with his shirt and rolled to his side to sit up.

"Maybe we should make it four so you're not the third wheel. Unless you plan on hanging out with Walsh at the life guard stand and leaving me and Ty in peace."

"Am I allowed to choose my own date?" David asked.

Anthony's forehead wrinkled in response. He texted Ty. Several minutes went by before he looked up with a guarded smile. "Yes. You're allowed. Ty's going to grab our suits and meet us there. She says we have to hurry."

David considered the texting conversation that had taken place and squinted at his best friend. "Scale of one to ten, how mad is she going to be if I ask Sophie?"

"I think she expects that." Anthony pushed his phone into his pocket.

"Is this about you and Sophie going out before? Or about Sophie trying to break you guys up?" David held off texting Sophie until he knew. Ty was his friend. Good friend. He didn't want to make her uncomfortable just because he wanted to spend more time with Sophie and get to know the woman who ate burgers at Red Robin and loved onion rings drowned in ranch.

Anthony followed as they headed for his car. "No. Not at all. Ty knows better than either of us that Sophie is far more into you than me these days."

"Then what's up?"

"Don't take this the wrong way, but she doesn't think Sophie deserves you. That's not how she'd put it, and I don't even think that's how it comes across in her head. She has this idea of the perfect girl for you, and Sophie doesn't fit it. More than anything else, she doesn't want you to end up hurt because you fall for Sophie without meaning to."

They got into the car, and David waited until they'd started down the street before he spoke again. "And what about you? You know me better than anybody else in the world. Is she wrong for me? Is this a bad idea to go down this road?"

Anthony shook his head. "There's a lot more to Sophie than I ever gave her credit for. You better text her now if you want her to come."

David nodded to himself, enthusiasm taking over. On the one hand, maybe Sophie was totally wrong for him. Maybe she wasn't though. He wanted to find out. He *really* wanted to find out.

He pulled out his phone.

DAVID

Ty's brother can get us into the Provo Rec Center for cheap this afternoon. Want to come?

The reply took longer than he expected.

SOPHIE

Uh. Sure.

DAVID

Great. We'll be by to pick you up in five minutes.

This time her reply came faster.

SOPHIE

Better meet you there. Gonna go buy a new swimsuit.

David wasn't quite sure what to think of that. He didn't want to be the hymn-singing guy, trying to fix Sophie, like Ty had first accused, or make her think she wasn't enough. But the fact that she was buying one? It made him feel good to think that she liked him enough to take his words to heart.

DAVID

You don't have to do that.

SOPHIE

Chill, bro. You're not that cool. I'm doing this for me.

David snorted with laughter and grinned anyway.

Sophie would have liked to take her time picking out a swimsuit. She took shopping seriously, and grab and go was not her style. In reality, she barely had enough time to run into Target, get a tankini top she could find that wasn't too hideous, and match up some bottoms.

When she met David at the Rec Center entrance, she swept his figure in one glance. It was only fair to pass judgment on his attire choices. Quid pro quo. In any case she didn't need much more than a once-over, considering he still had his T-shirt on and so no abs or arms to admire. Yet.

Then she saw his feet, which were encased in the dirtiest, ugliest Converse tennis shoes she'd ever seen.

She pointed. "What are those?"

"Shoes, Sophie. For someone who owns a million pairs at least, I figured you'd know something like that."

"Those are not shoes. I can't be seen with you wearing something like that." She waved her hand and scrunched her nose. "Who wears garbage like that to go swimming?"

"I was working with Anthony," he protested, reaching for her arm. Sophie let him take it and pull her closer. "I didn't have any choice. Ty brought our suits, and I waited out here for you. I haven't changed yet."

"Barefoot. That was an option."

He swung his arm around her neck and put her in a headlock. "That's enough out of you."

She laughed. David brought out the teen in her ... and she liked that. She'd bought a swimsuit because of things he'd said. The swimsuit she *wanted* to buy. David was right about one thing. Changing her natural choice didn't bother her like it had when she did it for Donavan.

When they met back at the deep pool after they'd changed, David didn't even look at her swimsuit. He watched her, his eyes holding hers, and not in a way that felt like he was avoiding looking at her body—but because he wanted to see *her*.

She spent the first few hours climbing the rock wall, playing tag on the empty tree house equipment for kids, and daring David to do ridiculous things as he rode the slides. After their second game of two-on-two water basketball, walking in the water was a chore, so she chose to lounge in a chair next to Ty while the guys raced to the top of the rock wall—again. She picked up her phone from the bag she'd staked out her chair with and dropped into her seat. No urgent e-mails, so she decided none of them needed to be answered right away.

It didn't surprise Sophie when Ty took up the topic of her and David. "So you and David have spent a lot of time together lately," Ty said.

"Yeah. He's fun to hang around." Sophie settled back in her chair and watched David and Anthony jostle each other near the top of the rock wall before they both fell off. They came up shaking their heads and wiping water from their faces and still wrestling good-naturedly. She knew they had grown up together like brothers and lived together since coming to BYU, except for the two years they'd spent apart while on their missions. So a future with David meant a future hanging out with Ty. Impressing Ty would get her another step closer to David. What did Ty think of her? Just another woman who'd wanted Anthony and lost?

"Are you guys ... dating? Or what?" Ty fiddled with the string on the front of her blue board shorts.

Sophie forced a laugh. "No. No, we're just friends. I'm not really David's type." She wanted Ty to contradict her. Ty knew David and what kind of girls he liked. She'd know if Sophie had a real chance of something more than flirting and friendship.

"Hmmm" was all Ty said. She studied a family sitting at the edge of the leisure pool with their baby, splashing in the shallow water. "Thanks for all you're doing for the wedding." She rolled her head back to face Sophie with a smile. "I know you did it for Anthony because you guys are ... friends." She ducked her head to hide a smirk. Even Sophie let out an embarrassed chuckle. "But thanks."

"You're welcome. Doing Anthony's wedding is good for my mom since he's so high profile. It's a win-win."

"Yeah ... you've probably already guessed, but I'm not a girl who planned her wedding growing up. Before I even met Anthony in person, I was set on marrying him, you know. Like those girls who all want to marry the One Direction guys?" She laughed at herself and shook her head. "But I never thought of it beyond that. He was just a poster on my wall. A guy out on the field while I was stuck in the stands. Even when Anthony and I started dating—and getting serious—I tried not to think too much about it. And I didn't even dream of planning stuff."

"Worried you'd jinx it?" Sophie guessed, studying Ty.

"He loves me. He'd never do anything to hurt me, but I can't help that little, tiny fear, right? The one that says he might bolt. But when you started pinning stuff to the wedding board? Then it got real. And exciting. And you're making my dream come true, even if you're doing it for Anthony." She held Sophie's gaze with that mockingly innocent smile. That must have reeled Anthony right in.

Sophie looked away, embarrassed. "Everyone deserves to have a dream wedding."

"Is that your mom's slogan?" Ty asked, giggling.

"It should be." Sophie enjoyed the surprising moment of friendship. "Have you decided on your dress yet?" That would be a great end to this day: David owing her ten bucks for Sophie predicting Ty's choice of dress.

"Um. Not quite. They're both so great. I never thought when you said that my choices would be limited because of my budget that you'd come up with two really, *really* great dresses. When do you need to know?"

"They'll need to be altered, so the sooner the better. But you don't need to rush yourself." The fact that Ty still loved them both didn't bode well for Sophie. She tried not to scowl. How could Ty want a dress she got lost in?

"I'll decide by tomorrow night. No ... the next night. Two

days. The deadline will be good. Otherwise I'll sit and stare at the pictures and go back and forth over and over." Ty set her mouth in a firm line.

"If you're sure …" Sophie's gut told her Ty wouldn't go her way, and her confidence took a hit. *It feels like the kind of dress a woman like me would get married in*, Ty had said about the Grecian dress.

"Yes. Boss me. Tell me you need an answer by Wednesday, no arguing."

"Uh. I need an answer by Wednesday. No arguing." Sophie couldn't help adding, "Unless you want until the end of the week."

"Way to be tough, Sophie. I know you better than that." Ty shook her head and then jumped up as the guys approached.

David jogged over to Sophie and grabbed her hand. "Come on. We're going to race down the lazy river now that that family got out. I can beat you for sure."

She shoved at him before allowing him to pull her along without analyzing Ty's opinion of her. Most likely Ty would disapprove of Sophie's crush on David, and that would ruin how fun it was falling for him.

Before David headed over to baseball practice the next afternoon, he went to Jay's apartment. David hadn't heard from Jay since he'd ditched the graduation picnic party. When he called, Jay ignored it. If David texted, Jay kept the conversation short. David didn't like forcing his company on Jay, but David had a responsibility to Noah and to Jay. Jay and Noah had been as close as David was to Anthony. David would never let Anthony give up on football and church without a fight. Noah couldn't do the same for Jay. That left it up to David.

"Grab your mitt," David said when Jay answered the door.

"I've got half an hour before I have to go to baseball practice. Help me warm up."

Either Jay didn't mind playing catch, or he knew arguing wouldn't sway David. He disappeared down the hall toward his room while David waited outside. Once Jay came back they headed for the same patch of grass.

"So, baseball practice, huh?" Jay did David the favor of starting a lot farther apart than they had their last game of catch.

"Figured I'd better go if I was serious about trying to play professional baseball. I'm not too bad. Should be right back up to par in a few weeks." They tossed the ball back and forth, waiting for their arms to warm up.

"Does that mean you decided to choose baseball over football?"

"No. Not yet. But I have to figure out if baseball is even a real possibility."

"If a recruiter is calling, he must think you still have it in you."

They started throwing harder, both of them inching back with every throw. "Yeah."

"What's holding you back? That girl you met?" Jay had to shout for David to hear him. Not the conversation he'd pictured.

"Sophie? No. Not really." They had fun together, but it was nothing serious, even if he wouldn't mind sticking around to find out if it could be more. Not knowing didn't help him make a decision, but it didn't hinder him from making one either. Either way, he had to leave Provo. "Just indecisive. Not sure what I want to pursue. Kind of like you."

Jay shook his head and didn't answer when he threw back.

"You thinking about your future at all? About going back to baseball ... or on a mission or whatever?"

Jay dropped his hand and let David's throw roll into the grass behind him. He pulled off his mitt, tucked it under his arm, and headed for his apartment. "Should have known you couldn't keep it to playing catch."

David ran after the ball first. "Hey. Wait!" Jay didn't stop, but he didn't hurry either. David caught up to him. "Did you really believe I'd let it go for good? Somebody has to ask you the hard questions."

"You think you're the only one who cares? Wow, how flattering."

"You're Noah's best friend, and he's worried about you." David put a hand on Jay's shoulder, but he shrugged it off and quickened his step, making it to the stairs that led to his apartment ahead of David. "If you knew something was wrong with him, wouldn't you want to help?"

"Tell Noah I'm fine. He doesn't need to worry." Jay took the stairs two at a time, but David didn't have any trouble keeping up.

"I'm not blind or stupid, Jay. You're not fine, and Noah has a good reason to worry."

Jay reached the door to his apartment and swung around. "What's that supposed to mean?"

"I've seen inside your apartment. So you don't want to tell me, whatever. I know what's keeping you from baseball and a mission, and it's a huge waste." David folded his arms across his chest. He didn't look down on Jay anymore, though he still had him by a few inches. It didn't stop him from thinking of him as a kid or doing what he could to intimidate him enough to listen.

"Not everybody wants to play baseball, or football or whatever, the rest of their life. Sure, I love it, but my chances of going pro like you were always slim, so who cares?"

"Doesn't make what you're doing okay. Partying and drinking are bad choices, plain and simple. Where are those things going to lead you? Not to any future you're going to like. Not any of the right places."

Jay pushed open the door, waving David off, not that it had any chance of working. He followed Jay inside.

Jay spun on David, leaning toward him, maybe in an attempt to intimidate him. "And what are the right places, Bishop?"

"Basic Sunday School answers, Jay. Church. Mission. Sealed to the right woman in the temple."

"You listened in Primary. Good job. Let me go get a sticker for you." He stood his ground, shaking his head and folding his arms. "I'm just having fun. That's what you're supposed to do in college. So let it go and leave me alone. I'm not a kid. I can make my own choices."

It didn't matter what David said anymore, but he still wanted to leave Jay with something he might remember when he was ready to listen. He backed off a few steps, toward the door. "Okay. Fine. But when you realize how the whole 'wickedness never was happiness' thing works, give me a call."

Jay snorted and shook his head.

"Later, then." David waved and strode out the door, failure nipping at his heels. What would he tell Noah now?

A couple grueling hours of baseball eased his anger at Jay rejecting all his efforts. Noah would tell him not to give up, and David had to agree. He needed to back off, though. Let his words sit with Jay for a while. In any case, he'd keep a prayer in his heart for Jay's benefit.

Half an hour after practice, Anthony and Ty were on their way to June Pope's office so Ty could make a final decision about her dress. Sophie had arranged for her to use the dressing room again to try on the dresses before she picked. She would do anything she could to make sure Ty chose the dress Sophie thought looked best.

Since the chance of seeing Sophie and maybe going out again brightened David's thoughts the moment it occurred to him, he talked Anthony and Ty into letting him tag along and even waiting while he took a quick shower. They stopped and picked up Ty's mom on the way. When she got into the back seat with David, Ty glanced back at them, grimacing.

"I must look like some kind of bridezilla, always bringing a bunch of people for the wedding dress stuff." Ty shook her head.

David was the odd guy out with no real reason for coming except to flirt with Sophie. "Don't worry. This is not a bunch of people. We don't even have Rosie with us this time," he joked.

That got a laugh from Ty. "Only because she had to work."

When they arrived at the offices, David looked around for Sophie immediately. Spending time with her had led to one thing for him: wanting to spend more time with her. He was falling, and he might have reached the point where he didn't care if he started a relationship with Sophie and then it went up in flames. Like at Red Robin, Sophie had relaxed when they'd gone swimming and just hung out with him.

But Sophie didn't meet them at the reception desk like she had the one other time he'd come with Ty. Instead the red-haired woman who had helped Ty with her dresses the first time stood up from behind another woman at the reception desk and greeted them.

"Welcome back. Sophie said you wanted another look at your two dresses. Come on back. They're waiting for you."

David's gaze roved the dressing room as they walked in, expecting Sophie to be standing there holding up the dress she wanted Ty to choose and insist she try it on first. She wasn't.

"Where's Sophie?" Thankfully Ty asked the question so David didn't have to, even though after two mostly successful dates, he didn't care what anyone thought of him seeking Sophie out.

"She couldn't make it in today, but she told me to make sure you had all the time you needed." The woman grabbed the dress Sophie didn't like and headed toward the dressing room.

"I'm sorry we're so late," Ty said to the woman, glancing at her phone before following her.

"Don't worry. I've got plenty of other stuff to keep me at the office late besides you. This is a busy time of year for the wedding business in Utah. I hope you don't mind me popping in and out while you admire yourself." She hung the dress inside and shut the door behind her and Ty, cutting them off from the conversation.

It would take a while for Ty to change—every dress had taken a while last time they came. And she wouldn't need his opinion anyway. He'd promised Sophie not to try to sway her one way or the other, so he slid out his phone.

> DAVID
>
> Where are you? You're the only reason I came to lend my opinion. That makes it your fault I have to endure this, and you'll have to make it up to me.

Ty had emerged from the dressing room by the time Sophie replied. David furrowed his brow. What had taken so long? Sophie kept her phone close at all times. He'd made fun of her for it the day before at the pool.

> SOPHIE
>
> Sorry. You know how bad I wanted to be there, but my stomach says otherwise.

> DAVID
>
> Your stomach?

> SOPHIE
>
> I feel like a truck ran me over a few hundred times. I'm down for the count. If you were my friend, you'd pour on the compliments when Ty tries on my choice.

> DAVID
>
> And lose ten bucks?

Ty was still twirling in front of the mirror, watching the skirt of her dress float around her. He turned back to his phone, but Sophie hadn't responded yet.

It took another twenty minutes to get a text back, and Ty had barely changed into the dress Sophie wanted her to buy.

SOPHIE

I am puking my guts out, David. Don't you feel bad for me at all? Make her choose the right dress.

"I'm never going to be able to choose," Ty moaned from in front of the mirror. She spun around. "Guys. What do you think? Honestly."

"I'm not sure why you brought me again," Kim said. "You know I think you look beautiful in both. I'm having just as hard a time choosing as you are."

"You look great in that one," David said. He gave her a thumbs-up and nodded encouragingly for good measure. Ty narrowed her eyes at him and turned to Anthony, who laughed.

"He's right."

"But which one is better?" she whined.

"That one, definitely," David said while typing.

DAVID

I promise I'm doing my part.

He snapped a picture of Ty in the dress for good measure. Maybe that would help Sophie feel better. Too bad he couldn't cook. He had the urge to make some chicken noodle soup.

Ty stood in front of the mirror long enough to give "time and all eternity" new meaning for David. Even though he hadn't gotten a reply yet from Sophie, he texted.

DAVID

You seriously owe me for not showing up.

"Can I try on the other one again?" Ty asked. The woman who had been helping Ty had poked her head in through the door. When had she left?

"Of course." She shut the door behind her and headed for the dressing room.

"I'm sorry. I don't mean to be so needy."

The woman waved it off. "It's your wedding day. Having the perfect dress is important." Both she and Kim went into the dressing room with Ty to help her change.

David's phone beeped.

SOPHIE

It's your own fault for going to watch her try on dresses.

DAVID

With the hope of seeing you.

SOPHIE

What a charmer.

"Glad you came?" Anthony interrupted with a wide yawn.

"Ecstatic. Remind me to stay away from all future wedding dress shopping events." He didn't look up as he answered.

DAVID

You know me so well.

SOPHIE

I need a SitRep.

DAVID

A what?

"Who you texting?" Anthony leaned over the arm of the couch.

"I'll give you three guesses."

Anthony laughed and flopped back onto his couch in time for Ty to come out wearing the Grecian dress, Kim and the assistant following. Kim gazed at Ty with glowing eyes. Anthony stood and walked toward Ty, hopefully to offer some words of encouragement and to get them out of this place.

SOPHIE

You're telling me a guy like you, who has probably watched hundreds of action movies, doesn't know what a SitRep is? Situation report?

DAVID

Okay, so I'm embarrassed about that. She says they're both crap.

SOPHIE

You are a terrible person. I'm sick.

DAVID

I'll bring you some soup later. Anything would be more entertaining than this. Even watching you puke.

SOPHIE

That is disgusting.

"Okay. You're right." Ty's words brought David away from his phone. She pulled Anthony's face down for a kiss. "This is the one. This is *the* wedding dress."

David hopped up. Truthfully, he'd never thought Ty would choose something other than what Sophie picked out. She had impeccable taste, and Ty did look amazing in the dress Sophie chose.

"Are you sure?" he asked, pocketing his phone.

"It's her wedding and her dress, Beast." Anthony shot David a glare followed by a pleading look. "She's beautiful in both, so it doesn't matter."

"Well, I'd better be the one to go tell Sophie." David started toward the door. What an excellent excuse to go to her apartment. She'd need comfort—after she paid up, of course.

"I can just call her." Ty frowned.

"This news is best told in person. Sophie was hoping you'd choose the other one." He backed away.

Ty turned to Anthony. "Maybe—"

"Time's up." He shook his head. "Your deadline has expired, and you made your decision. Now let's go celebrate by getting dinner."

She laughed. "Fine."

"See you guys later!" David waved and trotted out of the office.

"Beast!" Anthony caught up with him on the stairs. "Dude. You rode with us."

chapter twelve

HOW LONG DID it take a woman to get out of a wedding dress? And Anthony took his time, dropping Kim off before heading back to their house to drop David off. He and Ty sat in front, holding hands over the console, Anthony smiling at Ty as she chatted about how great the dress was and what an awesome wedding they would have. David sat in the back, staring out the window, resisting his need to ask Anthony to hurry up.

He hopped out of the car as soon as Anthony pulled up to the curb. "I love you two, I really do, but you're making me sick and jealous. Have a great evening!" He slammed the door shut on both of them laughing at him.

He went to Smith's first and picked up a carton of chicken noodle soup from their deli. He'd never had it before, but odds were it tasted better than anything he could make. He grabbed a chick flick from the Redbox kiosk outside and headed over to Sophie and Ally's apartment. He pictured the kind of date he'd been thinking about for a while. Sophie tucked into his side, her head on his shoulder, watching a movie and relaxing. A comfortable relationship he'd watched from the outside, wishing he was in.

He tapped on the door of Sophie and Ally's townhouse-style

apartment, trying to keep from shifting his weight side to side as he waited for one of the girls to answer.

"Come in!" someone called from inside. "It's unlocked."

David pushed the door open and peered inside the dark living room. "Sophie?" He glanced toward a lump on the couch.

"David?" A second later the blanket snapped over a mass of dark hair—Sophie's, David guessed—and her muffled voice asked, "*What* are you doing here? I told you how sick I am."

He walked to the couch and sat at what he assumed were her feet, since she'd hidden her entire body under a blanket. "I figured you needed someone to take care of you. I brought chicken noodle soup." He rattled the deli bag. "Isn't that what people need to feel better?"

"You're very sweet." She still hadn't pulled the covers from her face. "You can leave it right there." Her arm appeared from under the blanket, and she pointed at the shiny, metal coffee table she never let anyone put their feet on. "Thanks for coming by."

He set the soup on the table, but he didn't get up. "Why are you hiding from me?"

"I look awful. I can't allow you to see me like this."

"Seriously, Soph? We're friends."

"Exactly. I'm disgusting. A good friend would never subject you to something like that."

"A good friend came here to feed you chicken noodle soup and hang out with you tonight. I even brought a movie. You can sleep all the way through it if you want, but I'm not leaving."

"I'm not coming out from under this blanket. Which one of us do you think can be more stubborn?"

"You, I'm sure." He settled back against the couch. Waiting her out would take forever. He wouldn't give up this idea, though. It felt like a tipping point for them. That if he could convince Sophie to let him see her, this thing going on with them might be real. "So remember that conversation we had about how what I think has no bearing on how you look?"

It took a few seconds for her to answer. "Ye-es..."

"So prove it. What you wear doesn't matter, right?" he taunted.

"No, no, no. This is way different."

He chuckled at the fire in her voice. Proof right there. Whatever she was hiding under that blanket, she was still Sophie Pope.

"Hmmm. So you only expect me not to judge your appearance when you feel like you're pretty."

"You are evil."

He tugged at the blanket again. "Come on, Soph. I'm not going to care what you look like. I came to hang out and maybe watch a movie if you're up to it. Not to ogle, cross my heart."

It might have taken a full minute, but the blanket came down, revealing Sophie's face. Though pale, and maybe it struck him more because of her lack of makeup, she was still gorgeous. Prettier than any other woman he knew. Wide, almond-shaped eyes and heart-shaped lips—he knew them very well. Without makeup, her hazel eyes took center stage, and she even had the lightest smattering of freckles. She looked softer and vulnerable. Her hair, piled in a messy knot on top of her head, had strands falling out all over and sticking up every which way. And she wore a plain old T-shirt. She never wore regular T-shirts.

He sat there and stared at her until her jaw tightened and those amazing hazel eyes flashed. "Want to snap a picture?" she asked.

"Maybe." He started to grin. "Maybe it will remind me of the moment I decided you were the most beautiful girl ever."

The scowl dissolved into confusion, then wonder. It didn't take her long to come up with a comeback, but when she did, she whispered it. "You're so full of it."

He laughed and scooped his arm around her, pulling her close and laying one hand on the side of her face so he could stroke her cheek with his thumb. "I'm not joking, Sophie."

This time he didn't pull away when he knew they were going to kiss. This time he used his finger to tilt her closer to him.

She swallowed hard and laid a hand on his chest, making a feeble effort to keep them apart. "David..." she said in a low, scratchy voice.

He didn't let her stop him. They'd discuss whatever issues she had with kissing him later. After he'd kissed her. Better to ask forgiveness than permission.

She swallowed again. What could scare her about kissing him? One kiss? Did it really mean that much to her? He craned his neck, reaching for her lips.

The next second she puked on his shirt.

Sophie scrubbed at her teeth with a vengeance, spit out the toothpaste, rinsed, and then brushed her teeth for a sixth time. Perhaps she could salvage what probably would have been the best kiss of her life.

She spit again and glared at the mirror. After throwing up all over him? Fat, stinking chance. She stopped brushing her teeth long enough to splash water on her face and then ran her comb through her wet hair. Nothing pretty about her bedraggled appearance, even post-shower, but better than the sweaty, pukey mess she'd been before. She grabbed her toothbrush and went at it again.

As far as she knew, David sat downstairs waiting for her. He'd promised to stay and watch a movie even after she'd hurled partially digested saltine crackers on his shirt. She rinsed again, then wiped her hand over her clammy forehead and bent over the sink.

Who was she kidding? This was unsaveable. She pressed her head against the cool countertop. The way he'd gazed at her. None of the judgment she could swear she picked up when she wore something that showed more skin. She believed him when he'd said she was the most beautiful girl he'd ever seen. His eyes said it. His melty, dark brown eyes said that she, without a lick of makeup and resembling a zombie, was beautiful. He might have seen right into her soul. He thought she had a beautiful soul.

She swore.

"Sophie?"

David's voice surprised her. She whipped her head up so fast she wobbled and had to grab the counter with both her hands. He took one step across the room and grabbed her upper arms, pulling her against him to support her.

"You're not supposed to come up here," she said.

"I got worried. You've been in here awhile." He wrapped an arm around her waist and helped her to the door. "You done?"

"Yeah," she mumbled. As she leaned into him, she recognized the vanilla-cinnamon scent of the hand wash they kept in the downstairs half-bathroom. She giggled. "Mmmm. You smell delicious."

"Yeah, yeah," he said. "I did the best I could with the tools at hand. Thanks for the shirt, by the way."

She pulled back and scrutinized him. After she'd thrown up on him, he'd stripped off his shirt and rolled it up in the blanket before helping her up the stairs. Since she'd been concentrating on not throwing up again before she got to the bathroom, she hadn't been able to admire his shirtless top half again like she had at the pool a few days before. He'd hovered in the doorway while she bent over the toilet, humiliated that he was there to witness her like this, but touched all the same at the worried look on his face.

A few minutes later, when she was sure she wasn't throwing up again, she'd scrounged up what she'd thought was an enormous, misshapen T-shirt thrown into the stands at a high school basketball game years and years ago. She'd hurried for the bathroom and the shower again before he put it on.

But on David the shirt wasn't as enormous as she thought. Misshapen, yes. "Wow, Davey. That shirt is…"

"Super sexy?" he offered.

"Mmm-hmmm. Definitely."

She melted inside some more. What a great guy. Even now, when she must disgust him, he still stuck around to check on her. She glanced down at her clothes, a T-shirt and a pair of gray BYU sweats. Maybe he could be so sweet because he approved of her wardrobe choice today.

No, it was more than that. She'd pursued Anthony because he had so much going for him—a star football player, handsome, charming in the best possible way. But he'd also made her happy when she spent time with him, date, hanging out, whatever. He paid attention. He acted like a gentleman. He was happy with himself, and she'd wanted to be part of that. With David, it was all those things times a million, especially since he wanted her too.

He tightened his grip and headed out into the hall. She rested her head against his chest. "Your bed or the couch?" he asked.

She lifted her head to face him. "You still want to stay and watch that movie?"

"Of course."

"It would be kind of hard for me to watch it from my bed."

"Well, that's true."

"Downstairs then."

Once they reached the living room, the smell of Ally's citrus room spray hit Sophie full force. "You cleaned up," she said, shaking her head in wonder at him.

"Uh, most of it got on my shirt and the blanket. Hope you don't mind, I threw it all in your washer." He guided her to the couch.

"No problem." She leaned into him again.

He picked up a water bottle from the coffee table. "You should keep hydrated."

"Yes, sir, Dr. Davey." She rested her head against the pillow and gazed up at him. Okay, so he had opinions about her clothing choices, just like Donavan. Donavan had never brought her chicken soup. He would have freaked out if Sophie had puked on him. Judgments about her aside, David absolutely had more good-guy points than Donavan.

David leaned over close, closer than she would have dared to someone who had so recently puked all over her, his face inches away from hers. "That is a fabulous nickname."

She blinked lazily at him. Why did throwing up have to exhaust her so much? "I've heard lots of girls call you that."

"Those girls are not you."

"Where'd you learn to be so charming?"

"My mom, of course."

She laughed.

"You need anything else?" he asked.

"You going to tell me which dress Ty chose?" she asked.

David's expression froze. "That can wait until you feel better, can't it?"

Sophie could guess which one just by that answer. She just sighed and then smiled. This night had turned out too well for her to sulk over that right now. "Sure," she said.

He sat next to her and put his arm around her, pulling her close to him and gently kissing the top of her head. She sighed again. All puking aside, best date ever.

chapter thirteen

SOPHIE BENT over Ty's binder on her mom's desk, flipping through a few pages before going back to the schedule on her iPad. "Lunch with David," she murmured while tapping it in. Their first post-sickness date. She grinned until she saw the appointment after it: meeting Ty at *Impressions* for her first dress fitting. June had scheduled it for her.

It made sense. Sophie had taken over almost the entire wedding, with June supervising from backstage. Not much had gotten done the few days Sophie had called in sick, except for Ty choosing the wrong dress.

Sure, Sophie hadn't brooded over it when David first inadvertently told her. Sophie didn't brood over problems. She fixed them. Whatever Ty thought about the horrible Grecian goddess dress— Sophie checked herself. She'd liked that dress before Ty latched onto it and insisted she wear it for her wedding. Sophie couldn't let a client who thought she knew best, when clearly she didn't, make a bad choice like this.

But how could she get Ty to recognize that without telling her, straight up, that the dress didn't flatter her? Sophie tapped one of her nails against the screen as she tried to reason out a way to stop this train wreck before it ruined Ty's wedding for her. She'd look back on the pictures later and wonder why

Sophie hadn't done her job better. For the sake of Sophie's reputation and her mom's company, she had to get Ty to change her mind and choose the Jovi Roy dress.

In her peripheral vision, she caught sight of the notes from the wedding photographer June had worked out a deal with for Anthony and Ty's wedding. Maybe ... maybe if Sophie got him to do some preliminary pictures and show Ty how small the dress made her, she'd realize her mistake.

Sophie rubbed her hands together expectantly. She could even picture some soft, black-and-white shots of Ty in the *Impressions* dressing room. They'd be perfect to add to the wedding portfolio. Candid, real-life shots.

Sophie whipped out her phone and ran her finger along the photographer's page in Ty's wedding binder. She'd save this dress disaster and then some.

David waited next to her car when she came down a few hours later. She quickened her step. "I thought we were meeting at Café Rio."

"Couldn't wait." He reached out to put his hands on her waist and guide her closer.

"Not even ten minutes?" she teased.

"Nope. There's something about you, Sophie..." He shook his head at her, pretending to mull over what it could be.

"Like what?"

"Like your love of onion rings," he said. "And speaking of onion rings, there's something we need to get out of the way right now."

Sophie straightened up. He looked so serious, but beginning with *speaking of onion rings*? Where could that possibly lead? "And what is that?"

He pulled her even closer and rested his head against hers. In her heels, David only had maybe three or four inches on her. They fit so well.

"Something I've wanted to do for a while," he said almost against her lips.

"It's about time," she whispered back.

His lips pressed against hers. The kiss lived up to every single expectation she had. Curled her toes. Set flight a million tiny butterflies in her stomach. Left her needing more so badly that when he pulled away, her lips followed him and she gathered a bit of the sleeve of his T-shirt between her fingers, holding him close, before she remembered she was Sophie Pope and dropped back.

Still clutching his shirt, she took a long, deep breath. The smile their kiss left on his lips stretched wider. "Well." She cleared her throat. "Now that that's out of the way, where to for lunch?"

"My place?"

"Yeah. Great idea."

So thirty minutes later Sophie found herself sitting next to David on the couch in his living room, both of their feet resting on the beat-up, seventies-era, wooden coffee table (perpetually covered in soda cans, textbooks, and video game controllers), eating a peanut butter and jelly sandwich.

"I haven't eaten a peanut butter and jelly sandwich for years," she said.

He leaned his head back. "Seriously? You must have a way better food budget than I do."

"I have a better job than you do."

"I don't have a job at all."

"There you have it."

David studied her for so long she ran her fingers through her hair to ease her discomfort. "What?" she asked.

"I'm trying to picture you as a little kid. I don't see you eating PB and J then either."

"You'd have to ask my mom. I was a picky eater. I was a vegetarian for a few weeks in seventh grade until I realized I'd have to eat vegetables to be a vegetarian."

"Is that when your love of onion rings began? Because, hey, I'll eat any vegetable if it's battered and fried."

"And soaked in ranch."

"Amen, sister." They ate for a few more moments in silence till David spoke again. "You know—" he said with a mouthful of food and then stopped himself. She hid a smile behind her sandwich. Talking with a mouthful of food was one of her biggest pet peeves, but the fact that David had relaxed so much around her that his manners slipped? She didn't mind it so much.

He started again once he'd swallowed. "You know what I can't figure out? Why you almost married Donavan."

She shook her head and took a bite of her sandwich. "Guys ask about your ex, but they don't want to hear about them. Trust me."

"I'm serious. You and him. How did that work? You are your own woman, and you're determined—driven. For Ty to choose the right dress. Spending two years patiently pursuing Anthony and not giving up even when he was engaged—you've given up now, though, right?" She laughed and let him go on. "Why was Donavan something you wanted? I don't understand it."

"I thought we fit together. He was a great dresser—"

"No Converse All-Stars in his closet?" David wiggled his eyebrows.

That expression got her every time. Mischievous. Totally sweet and likable in all its innocence trying to look like a bad-boy. "No. He cared about how he dressed, and I thought that meant he had it together. And that the way he wanted me to look perfect all the time meant he cared about me. That he wanted me to put my best face forward to the world."

"No offense, Soph, but he sounds pretty shallow. All that matters is that you know who you are and what you can do." He stared hard at her.

"I do know who I am. Part of that is my love of clothes and

fashion." She stared hard back at him, wondering how to put into words what clothes meant to her. "Maybe I'm vain, but I love clothes, David. I *am* smart and confident. I enjoy figuring out how that translates to a great outfit. I shouldn't have to feel like people think I'm shallow because I'm wearing expensive shoes. Yes, Donavan was wrong to try and make me perfect, and I was stupid to think that meant he loved me—but that doesn't change that I like to dress pretty, and I think that's okay."

"Okay ... I suppose." His reluctant tone said he didn't agree, but arguing about her choices would ruin their lunch.

He picked up his milk, gulping it down and leaving a white mustache over his lip. She gave him a charmed-but-I'm-not-sure-why smile, reached up, and wiped it away with her thumb. He closed the distance between them slowly. The few, short kisses he left on her lips made everything in her hum with delight. He topped it off with a kiss on her nose before he pulled away. It didn't stop her from studying him. This guy. This guy! She'd thought she fit with Donavan because he dressed well and took her to nice places and showed her off, and she liked it. But giggling and burgers and PB and J fit so much more. She'd wasted the two years she spent trying to win over Anthony completely overlooking what she could have found in David.

The way he studied her sometimes, like now—gazing right inside of her with tenderness, and yeah, a bit of desire there too. He wanted her. He'd looked at her like that, all sweetness, the night she'd puked on him. No makeup. A mess. It hadn't mattered to him, and she fell for him more because of it.

When she thought the moment had reached its peak, he leaned forward and kissed her forehead. "I am so lucky you didn't marry Don." Laughter escaped her, despite the thoughtfulness behind his jab. "If you had," he continued, "he'd be sitting here with you, eating peanut butter sandwiches and you wiping off his milk mustaches, and that makes me more jealous than I can explain."

She set her sandwich down on the table and put her hands on

either side of his face. "Don't worry. Don would never eat peanut butter sandwiches. He hates the way the smell sort of lingers on you."

David grinned. "Like onion rings."

"Especially those."

He scooped an arm around her waist to yank her toward him.

Their noses smashed together as they kissed again, but it was romantic in the most unromantic way, making her insides swirl and spin and reel. And she loved every second of it.

chapter fourteen

BY THE END of the week, lunch at either of their apartments had become a habit. Sandwiches had never tasted so good, and Sophie had never laughed harder over a bowl of ramen noodles. David had tried to dress it up by adding canned chicken and peas. It'd tasted disgusting. They'd ended up dumping it in the garbage and going to Wendy's. Sophie *never* ate fast food, but she didn't care anymore. Not with David across the table from her brainstorming different ways to make ramen noodles gourmet, each sounding more ridiculous than the last.

"Back to your mom's office?" he asked when they got into his car. He rested his hand on the console and wiggled his fingers, his signal for her to hold his hand.

She slipped her fingers through his, running one along the callus on the pad of his index finger. "I have to go pick up flowers for a wedding we're doing tomorrow. Want to come? I'll need help unloading them all in the bride's backyard."

"Sorry, I'm busy." He gave her an apologetic kiss on the forehead.

He didn't have a job, and with his future up in the air, he'd told her he didn't intend to find one anytime soon. She tilted her head. "Oh, yeah? Doing what?"

"The guys and I have an epic *Just Dance* battle planned for this afternoon."

She swatted him on the arm, making him laugh. She widened her eyes, switching her minor glare into pleading. "Please? Can you picture me hauling boxes and boxes of flowers in these?" She lifted her foot and set it on the dash, exhibiting the divine, pastel-blue peep-toe pumps she'd worn that day.

"Maybe you should wear sensible shoes on days like today." He let go of her hand long enough to shift the car into gear and then grabbed it back up.

"And miss the pleasure of watching you admire my legs?" she teased.

"You're wearing pants today."

She playfully hiked the dark-wash trouser jeans past her calf and waited for David's reaction.

He didn't disappoint. Chuckling and focusing on the road, he started humming a hymn Sophie didn't recognize.

"I'm going to have to go shopping soon." She lowered her foot.

She couldn't help the tingle of excitement, though maybe she could attribute that to the electricity that always popped between her and David. Still, shopping. Any excuse to do that was okay with her. Changing up her style would be fun. New clothes. New possibilities. She had already scanned through Pinterest several times for new ideas.

He shook his head at her while he rubbed his thumb along the top of her hand. "If you want to shop for different clothes because they make you feel good, go for it."

"Um, thanks for the permission?" She waited for more but he didn't continue. "So please come with me to the flower shop? I'll have to go find other strong, muscled guys if you don't."

"Fine. I'll call Sean and postpone."

When they walked, hand in hand, into Eufloria, Sophie took a good long breath of the heady scents and leaned into David's shoulder. The bold purple flowers she'd always wanted in her own bouquet stood out among the others around them. With him at her side, she couldn't help wandering over to smell them. A round flower with tiny purple petals caught her attention. *Alium Giganteum*, the label read. She took out her phone and snapped a picture.

"You told me we came here to pick up flowers, not scout them." David bent over next to her as she took a close-up.

"These are fabulous. I want to remember them for when I plan my own wedding." Heat raced into her cheeks the moment she realized what she'd said. "Someday. And someone else might like them too. I am a wedding planner," she added in a rush.

He chuckled and squeezed her hand. "Didn't you have all this stuff planned once? With Don?"

She stood up. "Yeah, I hadn't quite gotten that far when he dumped me."

David's mouth dropped open. "*He?* Dumped *you?*"

Flattered delight shot through her at his flabbergasted gaping. "Yes. We were engaged less than two weeks."

"What an idiot." David shook his head.

"If you're talking about me, you'd be right. For going out with him for so long in the first place. And saying yes." She scooted closer and tipped her head back. She wouldn't mind a pity-kiss right now. David's Sir Galahad instincts were probably tingling.

"We all have our moments," he murmured, obliging her.

"Can I help you with anything—oh, sorry."

Sophie twisted to face the Eufloria employee and froze. She'd come to the store so often, scouting flowers for weddings, ordering them, picking them up, and she thought she knew everyone that worked there. But the last time Sophie had come by, Ciara Kelley hadn't been one of them.

"Sophie Pope," Ciara said flatly.

Holy cow, she'd cut herself in half. Still plenty curvy, Ciara played it up with wide-leg jeans and a shirt belted at her waist. Wow. She looked fantastic.

"You must be new here..." Sophie stammered. David glanced

between her and Ciara, probably wondering what had Sophie so unsettled. Talk about tingling senses—they were screaming at him now if the heat in her face told him anything.

Ciara's neutral expression rocketed into a hostile one. She folded her arms. "Oh. So now you're going to pretend you don't recognize me. Even if I have lost a lot of weight, it wasn't from my brain."

"No, no, no." Sophie held her hands up in defense. "I work with Eufloria a lot. I hadn't seen you here before, so I assumed you must be new, and it didn't come out right. Of course I remember you." She plastered on a fake smile, wishing it would slow down her mouth.

"What do you want?" If anything, Ciara's hostility increased. Not that Sophie blamed her, considering what she'd done. But they were adults now, not stupid teenagers. Couldn't Ciara cut her some slack?

"You look great," she offered.

"I know."

So much for easing the tension.

"I'm David, by the way." He reached forward and held out his hand. Ciara ignored it and instead gave him an appraising once-over. She didn't look impressed with him either, which shocked Sophie. Who couldn't be impressed with him? Confused, David dropped his hand. Maybe Ciara couldn't know how awesome he treated her or the way his tender looks could make her melt, but he was a BYU football player, and his smile was *something*.

"Yeah, you look like the jocks she always dated. Pretty but nothing upstairs," Ciara deadpanned.

Okay, wronged former schoolmate or not, Ciara didn't have the right to judge David like she knew anything about him. Sophie straightened and put her "professional hat" on. When she'd seen Ciara, she'd hoped to leave the shop less weighed down by guilt, but Ciara wasn't going to let that happen.

"I'm here to pick up the flowers for the Carr-Rowley wedding, unless you'd rather I went somewhere else."

Ciara clenched her jaw. Sophie was talking about one of the biggest flower orders she'd made at Eufloria this year, and if the shop had hired Ciara, she was good enough at her job to know that June Pope Weddings did a lot of business with them. Sending Sophie packing, as satisfying as it might be for Ciara, would also send *her* packing.

"Let me get someone to help you with that."

"Thank you." But Ciara had already whirled and stalked away.

"What was that about?" David asked.

"You don't want to know."

David pointed toward the doorway Ciara had disappeared through. "Oh, you two almost threw down, right here, and she called me a stupid jock. I definitely want to know what just happened." He folded his arms.

"I'm sorry about that. She hates me. That's not an excuse to treat you like that when she doesn't even know you, but I deserved it." She ran a hand along her forehead before resting it against his shoulder. Either she'd have to find a way to have a civil relationship with Ciara or Jessica would be doing a lot more flower runs than she wanted.

He rubbed his fingers soothingly along her back. "Sophie. Don't make me drag this out of you. How could she hate you?"

Sophie laughed and tilted her head back to look up at him. "Come on, you might be infatuated with me, but you know me better than that. There are people out there who don't like me."

"Okay, so you can come off kind of prickly sometimes, but hate?"

"If I tell you, you probably won't like me anymore. I'm not going to risk that." She sauntered toward the front of the store.

He grabbed her hand, holding her back. "Oh, no. You're not getting off that easy. Either you promise to tell me when we get in the car, or I'm going back to my *Just Dance* tournament and you can find someone else to be your muscle."

"That is a terrible threat. I don't believe a word of it."

He pulled her toward him and kissed her cheek. "See you

later tonight. I'll call Anthony and have him pick me up." He smirked, tossed her the keys to his car, and headed for the door.

She caught them out of the air, disappointed his back had been to her and he hadn't seen it. "You're going to leave me here to fend off Ciara myself?" she called after him.

"You don't need me to fight your battles." He waved over his shoulder.

"Get back here, punk."

He put his hand on the door and waited, his expression the picture of patience. Good grief, he drove her crazy in a way she couldn't resist. He stood up to her like most guys didn't, and yet he handled her gently at the same time.

"Fine. I'll tell you. But I'm going to be mad when you dump me over it, and that 'fury of a woman scorned' bit? It'll seem tame compared to me." She had to at least sound in control of this thing going on between them.

He returned to her side and kissed the end of the finger she pointed at him. "I'm not worried. I doubt it's half as bad as you're making it out to be."

"You'll see."

David didn't press Sophie about her confrontation with the florist until he'd finished helping her unload the flowers in the enormous backyard of Quinn Carr, the owner of a well-known chain of department stores, who'd hired June Pope Weddings to give his youngest daughter an over-the-top reception.

"Okay, spill it," David said when she climbed in the passenger seat and shut the door behind her.

"I'd hoped you'd forget." She sighed. She sat back and turned toward him. "Short story? I ruined her prom dress the night of our senior prom."

David waited. When she didn't continue, he said, "There has

to be more than that. I know girls can be crazy about prom dresses and everything, but that isn't enough to cause the hate that girl radiated."

Sophie chewed on her lip. She couldn't think he'd actually break up with her over something that had happened in high school, could she? Even if Sophie had been twice as bratty as he already suspected, she was twenty-three now. Plus, genuine guilt had crossed Sophie's face back at the flower store. Whatever had happened with the prom dress, how much her actions in the past bothered her showed in the way she hugged one arm across her stomach and stared at the console between them.

She closed her eyes. "My boyfriend, the quarterback, no less, asked her to the prom two days after he broke up with me and left me dateless."

"For how long?"

She opened her eyes and scowled at him. "How long what?"

"How long before you had another date?"

That brought a little smile back to her face. He reached over and kissed her, just to reassure her. Sophie might be a higher-maintenance woman than he'd ever dated before, but he'd never had this much fun. He wasn't giving her up unless she confessed to murder. For heaven's sake, she'd choked down three bites of his ramen noodle disaster before he made her stop.

"Well?" he asked, taking her hand and kissing the top of it.

"How am I supposed to concentrate with you acting like that?" He shrugged. She took a breath and continued. "Okay, so I had another date by the next day, but I was shallow then, and I couldn't fathom why he'd ask *her.* I was furious." She took another deeper breath. "Preston kept all the same plans as we'd had, so that made me even angrier. She was on the decorating committee, and when I came to pick up the crowns for the night, her dress was in her car in the parking lot. I think she was planning on getting ready at a friend's house or something after they finished the last of the decorating. Anyway, my friends and

I got into her car and destroyed it to get back at her for going to prom with Preston—who, I might add, I found out she'd had a huge crush on for years." Sophie swallowed and looked over at him, like she expected him to hop out of the car and run away. Truth was, he had a hard time not bursting into laughter. Yeah, she'd been the mean girl and wrecked some girl's prom, but it had happened years ago. David had expected much worse considering the way both girls had acted.

"I can overlook it."

"It's worse. Preston only asked her because a bunch of guys dared him to. So the whole thing was a disaster."

"That part isn't your fault." He put his arm around her to pull her closer to him.

"As evidenced by her treatment of you today, she sees it differently." Sophie sighed.

"Okay, time for some hard truth, sweetie." He gripped her shoulders so she faced him. "It happened in high school. Sometimes people are mean in high school. Someday she may forgive you. Today isn't that day. But that's her problem, not yours, so you have to let it go."

"Just like that?"

"It's not 'just like that' for you. If I had to guess, I'd say you've volunteered at that prom dress thing trying to make up for it."

She gave him a small smile, contentment showing in her face. "It doesn't feel much like penance anymore. I like it too much."

"That has to be some kind of sign, right? You've paid your debt. Don't worry about it anymore." He dropped his hands and took one of hers in his again.

She examined them, tracing invisible lines. "So I take it you're not breaking up with me over it?"

"Not a chance. You didn't think I really would, did you? Over a prom dress?" Girls were unfathomable sometimes. He started the car. "We've had a hard day. How about we stop off at that great cake shop?"

"*We've* had a hard day?" she asked as he pulled out of the long, circular driveway.

"Did you see all those boxes of flowers you made me unload?"

He caught Sophie peering at him with amusement. He answered it with a grin of his own. Life was good.

chapter fifteen

"HOW DID PICKING up the flowers go?" June asked when Sophie came back to the office after her hour-long cake-eating break with David.

"Fine." She wouldn't bother her mom with the details about Ciara. Even if David thought Sophie should let the past go—and she had held on too long—she still needed to figure out how to not have a showdown with Ciara every time she had to go to Eufloria.

June tipped forward in her chair and rested her elbows on the desk. "I've been meaning to tell you, sweetie, how happy you look. I'm glad things are working out with David. He seems like a great guy."

"He is." Conviction fluttered around in Sophie's chest. He really was something. He took care of her, and maybe they had some differing opinions, but maybe it was because he cared about her, not that he was making judgments. "And I feel happy with him."

"It's showing." June reached across her desk to squeeze Sophie's hand. "In everything. Your work on the Rogers-Daws wedding. Your new look."

Sophie frowned. "New look?"

June's smile turned careful. "The lack of short skirts..."

Sophie frowned thoughtfully as she sat in the chair across from her mom. "I know I push the limits, and before I didn't think it was a big deal, but around David I feel a lot different. He doesn't treat me like Donavan did. I'm not a prize to him."

"Sophie." June paused for a long time before going on. "How you dress is the outward way of saying how you expect people to treat you. With Donavan, you dressed like his prize. Hopefully you dress differently with David because you feel differently."

Sophie took in a deep breath, unsure of what to think. There had always been a difference in the way she'd dressed on campus and away from campus, but she'd never worn anything too scandalous. But what did that style say about her? It said she was comfortable with her body when so many other girls weren't, that she liked herself. But what if her short skirts and tank tops said something else? What if it had been about being a prize, being looked at, and being admired?

June bit her lip. "I'm proud of you sweetie, whatever the reason. You've been having more fun with life, but also recognizing your responsibilities here and as an adult. I don't know if that's David, or you graduating, or what. I like it, and it's making you happy, so go with that."

The words tumbled around in Sophie's head, and she leaned forward again. "Why didn't you ever say you didn't like the way I dressed?" she asked.

June burst into laughter. "Oh, Sophie, you have a short memory. I gave up arguing with you about the clothes you wore a long time ago. We fought too much."

Sophie opened her mouth to retort but couldn't think of a reply. She and her mom *had* fought a lot until Sophie started her senior year of high school, and more often than not about the length of Sophie's dress for a dance at school or the tank tops she wore around in the summer.

"I figured you'd have to decide for yourself if you were going to change," June said, interrupting Sophie's thoughts. "And you did." Another smile split her face.

"Sophie?" Kaylie, the receptionist, interrupted by poking her head in the door. "There's someone here to see you. I had him wait in the extra office."

Sophie popped up, wondering if it was David and why he'd come back. She couldn't think of any other guys who would come by the office. Grooms usually left the wedding planning business to the brides.

"Thanks." She followed Kaylie out, pausing by the door. "Thanks for the compliments, Mom."

"You deserve them, honey. You worked hard for them." June waved.

When Sophie walked into the extra office and the devil himself sat in one of the white club chairs, she stumbled back against the door.

"Donavan?" Were her eyes playing tricks on her?

He confirmed his identity by checking her out in true Donavan style—a long once-over as he critiqued her clothing choices. Anger started to burn in her stomach at the way his face pinched together.

"You never looked good in wide jeans, Soph. It makes you frumpy," he said when he finished evaluating her.

Sophie closed and opened her fists. "Hello to you too."

He laughed and stood. "Don't get so upset. I'm trying to help you out. Like always."

"There are quite a few people who'd tell you I don't need your help when it comes to style. I've gotten along fine without you. Why are you here?" She stayed near the door and folded her arms, hoping whatever he came here for would take him away as suddenly as he'd arrived.

He flashed his almost-a-leer smile and pointed at her with both index fingers. "You."

She backed up another step. "Already dumped your latest fiancée? Thanks, but no thanks."

He slipped his hand into his pocket and then held out a card for her. "Not quite what I meant."

She inspected the card. A gorgeous, blonde-haired, blue-eyed woman in the background caught her attention. It looked like the woman Sophie had seen Donavan with at the cake shop. Bold writing along the top said "MormonMixer.com" and listed Donavan and another guy as the founders.

"What is Mormon Mixer?" she asked.

"It's a social media site for Mormons." Donavan settled back into the chair.

Still scrutinizing the card, Sophie settled onto a matching couch across from him. "*Hot* Mormons," she read off the tagline and set the card down on the table between them.

"It's a place where *normal* guys and girls can find a date without sifting through all the people stuck in their parents' basements or the girls desperate to get married."

"And what do you want from me?"

"We're partnering with a local station to do a mini dating show. We'd do short spots showing Mormon Mixer site users meeting and follow the relationships of a few. We need a host and someone to help us brand the company. You. You're perfect for the job. As long as you leave your baggy jeans at home." He chuckled to himself.

Sophie picked up the card and studied it again. Doing anything to help Donavan get ahead disgusted her, but he'd hit upon the one thing that tempted her. The opportunity to work on a real TV show? Get her name out there by helping launch a successful business?

She looked up at Donavan again. "Why me?"

He had his pitch ready. "Because you're usually put together. You project confidence, and you're beautiful. Exactly the type of people we want on Mormon Mixer."

Beautiful. She lifted her chin. When she'd dated Donavan, she would have ached for a compliment like that from his lips. Her eyes strayed to the blonde in the background of the card. She probably felt the same.

Anger snapped inside of her, despite how tempting the

spokes-woman idea sounded. For anyone but Donavan she would have jumped to know more. "I think you're looking for a Barbie doll, *Don*." She relished the way his eyes narrowed when she used David's nickname for him. "Someone you can dress up and who will do what you want. I'm not that girl." She stood up, wanting to get out of this room, out of the vicinity of Donavan. She tossed the card on the table in front of them.

He reached up and grabbed her arm, which she immediately jerked away. "Think about it, Soph," he said in a smooth voice. "You're walking away from being the star of your own reality TV show. Think of what that means."

She ground her teeth together and took another step away for good measure. The problem was she liked this spokeswoman idea. Really liked it. The dating show sounded like others she'd watched before—except instead of one guy dating a bunch of girls, this one would focus on real, one-on-one relationships. Admittedly, these would be relationships that started out on a site populated by mostly shallow people like Donavan, but there had to be some normal people on there.

But for Donavan? A guy who put too much importance on perfection in his relationships? Was that the type of guy qualified at all to help other people find "perfect" love?

On the other hand, it was experience, and he'd said the shows would appear on a local station. With host and PR experience on her résumé, Sophie could get a foot in the door of local television. Or get her start freelancing in public relations.

"Think about it?" Donavan picked up the card and handed it back to her. She pressed her lips into a thin line but took it. "We start filming the first few dates next week. We'd like to have you on board."

She didn't pay attention as he left. Settling back into her chair, she studied the card for a long time.

David tapped his phone against his arm, annoyed that he still didn't have an answer from Jay after texting him an hour before. He'd given up hope after the last few times without an answer, but Jay had to give in sometime, didn't he? Two weeks had passed since they'd argued at Jay's apartment, and Jay still hadn't cooled off enough to take David up on playing catch again, even with promises that David would keep his mouth shut. He needed to check up on him. Be there in his life.

Annoyed, he sent another message.

DAVID

Still too mad at me for calling you out, then?

To his surprise, Jay answered this one.

JAY

The wicked take the truth to be hard.

David chuckled.

DAVID

Snap. Good one.

JAY

Surprised that someone who isn't as perfect as you can quote scripture?

He frowned at the text. Perfect? David? Far from it.

DAVID

Never said I was perfect. Do I have to be to tell you to care about your life?

JAY

Ha. I know you think you're better than me. I'm cool. Like I said, you're not the first one to want to talk to me about this. Just don't be so shocked I don't want to hang out.

It took David several minutes to figure out what to text back, but it didn't matter since Jay didn't reply again. So David glared at his phone and tried to understand why Jay would say that about the way David acted. Better than him? It brought to mind a few comments over the last few weeks that stuck out to him now. Dallas Cooke's attitude about David's date with Katie and going to the NFL. The stuff Sophie said about him judging her. And now Jay.

He went back to tapping the phone against his arm, eyes narrowed in thought. Why *did* he ask Sophie to dress differently? Because he wanted to show her that her self-worth didn't depend on how sexy she was?

Or because he thought he knew better what the right choices were?

With Jay it was so much more black and white. Jay had made some dumb choices, choices that *would* lead him down a dark path regardless of whether David was wrong for judging or not. But maybe he just needed to be there for Jay. He'd said his piece.

He dialed Jay's number, and it didn't surprise him when Jay didn't pick up. He left a brief message. "I'm sorry, Jay. Let's get together sometime to play catch. Just catch, cross my heart." He hung up and let out a long, low sigh laden with failure.

Scowling, Sophie attempted to smooth down the fly-away hairs on her crown, trying to make them fit in with the waves around them. When that didn't work, she gathered her hair up into a pony tail and fixed a messy bun at the back of her head, hiding the curls she'd spent the last hour perfecting. She had too much to do today to worry about bad hair, starting off with an appointment with Ty. Armed with the pictures from the fitting, Sophie was prepared to talk her out of the drop-waist Grecian and into the sleek, exquisite Jovi Roy design. Sophie even had Jessica keep it in the dressing room in preparation for her victory.

The debacle with her hair made her late getting to the office.

"Ty is waiting in the extra office," Kaylie said as soon as Sophie walked through the doors.

"Thanks." Sophie headed straight there, digging the package of photos out of her purse as she strode toward the room. She wanted to get the dress change out of the way so she could call someone from Jovi's office and get Ty in for a fitting as soon as possible.

Ty looked up from the magazine she was reading when Sophie walked in. "Good morning."

"Hey. Sorry I'm late. Hair problem." Sophie sat in one of the club chairs, set her purse down beside her, and put the package of pictures on the table between them. "Look what I have. Pictures from your fitting." She pulled the stack out and spread them before Ty, waiting for the inevitable scowl as she realized how silly she looked in the dress.

Ty's expression was unreadable as she ran her fingers above the pictures then leaned down to study them. "These are..." She sighed. Here it came. The confession that Sophie had been right all along and Ty had chosen the wrong dress. "These are so cool."

"Don't worry—what?" Sophie scowled. "Well, yeah, Evan did an amazing job catching some good moments." Sophie could admit that. "But—"

"I love this one. Seriously. I need a print of this one." Ty held up a proof of her holding out the skirt in front of the mirror, that same dreamy expression drifting over her face, like every time she'd tried on the dress. She'd tilted one shoulder toward the mirror. The perfect image of a little girl playing dress-up and longing to be a princess.

Yeah, Sophie had to admit the shot captured an endearing moment, but that was beside the point. Ty couldn't look like a little girl playing dress-up at her wedding, and these pictures hadn't done the job Sophie expected.

She'd have to convince Ty head on, be upfront and honest about the way that dress fit on her. Sophie could bring up how Ty had signed a contract with June Pope Weddings and that

Sophie couldn't let her do something that would reflect badly on the company—how would the advertising they got out of this work if the dress was all wrong? She wanted Ty to make the decision to change dresses herself because she saw which dress was best. But Sophie's well-founded argument hadn't brought Ty to that conclusion. Sophie took a deep breath and prepared to dive in.

"I have to be honest with you, Ty, I'm still not convinced this is the best dress for you."

Ty's head came up from the pictures, confusion clouding her eyes. "I know you like the other one better..."

"I do. This one," Sophie tapped the pictures still on the table, "makes you look like a little girl. The drop waist is all wrong for your petite figure. It accentuates how short your legs are and shortens them even more." Sophie reached back into her purse and pulled out her secret weapon: an enchanting picture of Ty in Jovi's dress. Well, Sophie hadn't edited it to look nostalgic, the way Evan had with the others, but it worked anyway. The dress flowed over Ty's petite figure and lengthened it out. Sophie needed that visual for her offense.

"See how elegant you are in this one." She put the picture on top of the others. Ty's gaze lowered, along with her eyebrows and the corners of her mouth. Ty would understand how much better this dress was for her. Sophie dressed brides all the time, as far back as high school. June used to bring home pictures of dresses and brides all the time for Sophie's opinion, and no one had ever ignored her suggestions. Why would they? She made them look fabulous, and didn't all girls want to look fabulous on the biggest day of their life?

She drew another breath and forged on. "The higher waistline elongates your legs and creates the illusion of a tall figure. You'll look so fantastic next to Anthony in his tux. Instead of looking like a child next to him, you'll look like a lady. A tall, gorgeous lady." Sophie beamed. How could Ty resist that argument?

Ty pushed aside the picture and picked up the print of her in front of the mirror. She bit her lip then lowered her voice. "I look like a little girl?"

Sophie opened her mouth to keep fighting, despite the wiggle in her stomach at the sad sound of Ty's voice. Sophie might have gone too far in saying Ty looked like a child. She would tone it down.

Ty stood up, stopping her with a hand. "You're right. You have been all along. I should wear the other dress."

Sophie jumped up, confused about why Ty was leaving. "Great! I can call Jovi, and we'll get you right in for a fitting. I bet we could get it done this morning."

Ty moved toward the door. She waved her hand, too quickly to come off as nonchalant. "Uh, not this morning. I can't. Maybe tomorrow? Or the next day. I know you need to get this moving along. I understand, but I can't." She put her hand on the door and opened it.

"We have some other things to go over." Sophie frowned and took a couple steps toward Ty. What was going on? Shouldn't Ty be happy that Sophie worked hard to get the best for her? That she'd discovered how silly she looked in the other dress before it was too late?

"Oh, right. Can we reschedule that? Thanks." She disappeared through the door before Sophie could stop her.

Sophie tried to shrug off the guilt coiling in her stomach. Changing her mind now when she'd fallen in love with the Grecian dress might upset Ty, but when she put the Jovi one on again she'd get how right Sophie had been.

She gathered up the photos and stuffed them back in her purse before heading over to her mom's office. She had a lot of things to shuffle around to get Ty in tomorrow and reschedule the planning they needed to do. She had to get started.

chapter sixteen

SOPHIE'S DAY didn't get any better after that. Jovi couldn't get Ty in for a dress fitting until the end of the week, which would put any alterations behind schedule as well. That would cut things close, and Jovi wasn't keen on the idea of pushing her seamstresses to work overtime for a dress they were barely making a profit on, even if Rocket Rogers's bride was wearing it.

Sophie decided to head straight for David's after working late and get some comfort cuddling in. With any luck, he could advise her on Donavan's offer, since Sophie couldn't make a decision about it on her own. Donavan had presented her with the opportunity to be in the public eye, but the thought of working with him made her skin crawl. Talking it over would help her separate the good in the offer from the things that held her back. Like the fact that Donavan had a partner. Maybe the partner would be easier to work with than Donavan. And the people from the TV station couldn't be all bad either. If she could somehow limit her interactions with Donavan, the offer would be all but irresistible.

Anthony answered the door when she knocked, which, after her encounter with Ty, made Sophie uncomfortable.

"Is David here?" she asked.

He nodded curtly and held the door open wider. David sat on

the couch and glanced at Anthony. Sophie almost backed away and fled. Anthony was annoyed with her, probably over what had happened that morning with Ty. Had their talk upset Ty more than Sophie realized?

"Is now a bad time?" She hovered in the doorway.

David got up. "Nope. Come on in, Soph."

She stepped inside, avoiding Anthony's glare as he stood with the door open.

"I'll see you two later." He left, closing the door behind him.

"That was nice of him to give us some alone time," Sophie said, grimacing at the door before heading toward David. She wrapped her arms around his neck and breathed in his comforting scent, a cheap cologne mingled with his laundry detergent.

"He's, uh, not very happy with you right now," David said into her hair.

She pulled away enough to look up at him. "About the dress thing?" Why was it even a big deal?

"About forcing Ty to change her mind."

Sophie pulled away from him. "I didn't force her. I showed her why it would be better to choose Jovi's dress. She looks a lot better in it. She'll thank me when she sees her wedding portraits." Sophie had pictured winding down at David's with more cuddling and kissing and far less irritation.

He put his hands in his pockets and rocked back on his heels. "Why couldn't you let her choose herself? Isn't it more important for her to be happy than for the pictures to look good?"

Sophie clenched her jaw. "It's not just about the pictures looking good. That dress she chose isn't a little wrong on her. It's a lot wrong. People will notice."

He shook his head and dropped onto the couch, staring at his hands and rubbing them together. "Since your business is weddings, you know more than me, but the only people that it really matters to are Anthony and Ty. It's their day."

Shaking her head, Sophie backed closer to the door. "Not

this wedding. Yes, I'm the one who offered it at such a low price, and I had a dumb reason for doing it, but Anthony and Ty agreed to use everything for publicity for the firm in exchange for the price my mom gave them. The wedding photos, their story, everything is being used for advertising in some way. If we can't even make a bride look good, why would someone hire us?"

David sighed. "I get that, but it's still her day. She's upset, so Anthony is mad."

He meant it as a peace offering, but she couldn't take it. "What am I supposed to do, David? We're talking about the reputation of my mom's company. Brides that come to us expect the best."

"I understand, Sophie, but—"

"You don't, or you wouldn't argue with me about it. I'm sorry, but maybe hanging out with you wasn't a good idea. It's been a bad day, and with Donavan's job offer on my mind, I thought I could relax."

He stiffened. "Job offer? You have a great job working for your mom for a while. Why would you work for Donavan?"

"He and a friend founded a website that's getting big. They're doing a dating show on a local TV station to advertise their business. He wants me to host and work on the PR for it." She waited for David to make an objective observation about it. She needed him to. Even though she hated that Donavan was a part of the package, she hadn't been able to stop thinking about the possibilities. The restaurants they could feature to draw in the audience. Fashion spots where they could show off some great local boutiques she knew of, and maybe even Sophie sharing her knowledge about dressing for body types—taking her Dream Dress Project hobby to a whole new level. He was awful, but Donavan could make it happen because of what he offered. If David could support her, she could make it through working with Donavan. She could survive the critical comments that would come with it and the fighting she'd have to do to make him see how valuable she was.

But David clenched his jaw. "What kind of website?"

They shouldn't talk about it now on the heels of an argument, but the challenge rose up in her anyway. Who was David to tell her how to do her job? And now, who was he to stand in the way of her dreams? She dug the card out of her purse and held it out to him.

Still glaring, he took it, his expression changing to disgust. He smoothed it out and shook his head. "I'm not sure I understand what there is to consider."

She snatched the card back. "Getting excellent experience at a promising company. My face on a local TV station. Recognition if I decide to start my own firm. And possibilities, David. A lot of possibilities."

"By hawking a website for beautiful people only."

That did it. The worries she used to have about David's criticism flared back up and flew out of her mouth. "This would be so much easier for you if I were ugly, wouldn't it? So much less to judge about me." She stuffed the card back into her purse and folded her arms.

His mouth dropped in confusion. "What? No. I don't care about your looks one way or the other."

She'd thought that too, that maybe all his talk about who she was on the inside meant something. But if it did, shouldn't he support her in getting out there and making something of herself?

"Really?" she said. "Because according to you the way I present myself is distracting, and you'd rather I wore muumuus and turtle-necks. Which should have been my first warning sign, since Donavan always told me how to dress and act too. It's like you're the opposite of him but still wrong."

David stared at the ceiling for several seconds before he answered. "What I think about the way you dress shouldn't matter, and I never should've made it a thing. I just wanted you to know your worth, Soph. That's on me, I get it. But *that*?" He pointed to her purse, which held the card. "That is Donavan saying that you—or any woman—is meant to be seen. That the number-one priority when finding someone to marry is how physically attractive they are. That your talents are all about how sexy you look. Instead of how talented you are—your eye for finding the best in people, the fact that you can't help but fix everything. Why would you go back to Donavan and let people judge you for how you look instead of what you can do? Why would you promote something that would make others feel the way Donavan made you feel?"

She swallowed hard. Confusion and anger welled up inside her. Who cared what the website did or didn't do? Sophie wanted to growl a cutting response at him, but she couldn't speak through her emotions. He watched her warily. Finally, she spoke, forcing her voice to sound level. "This is a golden opportunity, David, that's the point. So maybe I'll have to put on a show to placate Donavan, but I can use what he's offering to make big things happen."

"So you'll sell yourself short in order to open a few doors?" David tilted his chin down and frowned.

The disappointment in his face twisted her insides in painful ways that left her vulnerable, the same way Donavan scrutinizing her before he'd give her a compliment had affected her. Why had she spent so much time trying to please guys who didn't think she was good enough? Time to stop.

She reached for the door handle. "I'm done trying to measure up to impossible standards. I like myself. I'm comfortable in my skin. I changed my style to humor you because we were having fun. Not anymore." She swung open the door and pushed at the screen, reaching the top step before David rushed to the door.

"I never asked you to be something you're not." He grabbed for her hand.

She shook away, refusing to allow his magical charms to dissuade her. "You're disappointed every time I'm not what you want, though." She hurried down the steps and toward her car as fast as her heels would carry her, which, considering how adeptly she ran in heels, was pretty fast. Good thing. For some stupid reason tears had formed, and by the time she pulled away from the curb, catching sight of David running up the sidewalk in his bare feet, fat drops rolled fast down her cheeks.

No matter how many times David went over his argument with Sophie, he couldn't figure out how to fix things. Even if he'd fallen hard, he couldn't date a woman who devalued herself so much just for opportunities.

Was he making too big a deal out of the job with Donavan? He went to his room to retrieve his laptop. He should have gotten more information about it before arguing against it, but the thought of her back under Donavan's thumb made his insides burn. Once he had the internet browser up, he typed in the site name he remembered from the card. As he scrolled the site and checked out some of the profiles, his conviction that he was right in questioning Sophie's role grew.

The website users were way-above-average–looking people, and everything emphasized looks. Dyed hair, overdone makeup, guys using more product than a guy ever should. Still stung by Sophie's accusations that he'd judged her for her looks and would prefer her to be less attractive, he forced himself to reserve judgment until he dug deeper. But the online conversations he read as he browsed the pages and profiles didn't improve his opinion. Most were concerned with fun and no interest in lasting relationships. The site description even touted that you could discover an edgy side of Mormons you never knew existed.

Donavan had created a site all about a bunch of people pushing the limits and acting shallow, and Sophie was considering representing that for the sake of recognition and the experience. And she wanted to deal with Donavan to do it? He pushed his laptop away and sighed. Maybe he'd made her into his idea of the perfect woman. And maybe she wasn't the woman he thought he'd fallen for. Was that Sophie a dream he'd seen through rose-colored glasses?

The part of him falling in love with that woman had run down the sidewalk after her and told himself that when they both had a chance to cool down, he'd go to her house and talk this out with her. But if he loved a woman who didn't exist, that was a moot point.

He clicked open his e-mail. He hadn't answered Noah's last letter since he didn't have anything to report, but he could sure use his brother's inspired advice on what to do with his life. He typed out an overview of his fight with Sophie, being honest about his reservations. Then he added to the end, *Haven't made any progress with Jay either. I'm trying to sit back and wait him out, but Jay can be pretty stubborn. I keep thinking about the trouble he could have gotten into since we last talked. I know you're praying for him. Keep it up.*

Unloading his problems had lightened David's grim view of the situation more than he'd expected. He left the argument with Sophie in the e-mail for now, and it weighed on him a little less. He shut his laptop and went to bed.

chapter seventeen

SOPHIE CALLED Donavan when she got into the office on Wednesday morning. He told her the first show was scheduled to film that Friday evening at a local club. She'd have to talk to her mom and shuffle around some reception responsibilities she had for another wedding, but she could do it.

No worse than walking away from the best relationship she'd had in years.

She hung up the phone and shook that thought out of her head. She hadn't given up David for Donavan. That would be stupid. She'd given up David because he couldn't stand behind her when she opened the doors that opportunity knocked on. He'd said she could do anything she wanted; he'd said she should get what she wanted, but when the time came for her to do that, he'd turned away.

"Good morning, sweetie. You're here early." June glided into the office and dropped a couple binders on the desk.

"I have a lot of things to go over before I meet with Ty this morning." She picked up the binder she'd been working with before calling Donavan and vacated her mom's chair for her, settling back down in one of the chairs across from her desk.

June didn't move, though. She leaned against the big desk and took a breath. "I'd better take over the Rogers-Daws wedding from here, Soph. You may be ... expecting too much from it after you talked me into giving them such a large discount." She punctuated this shocking news with a forced, overly sweet smile.

Sophie stood up, blinking away more tears. She and David hadn't even been that serious, yet ever since walking away from him, she couldn't keep her emotions at bay. "I've worked so hard to make this the most fantastic wedding this office can produce, and you're going to kick me out just like that? Is this about the dress? Did Ty tell you I forced her to choose Jovi's dress? Because I didn't. I pointed out that—"

June's face went from placating to stern within seconds. "Sophie, I know you're right about the dress, and Ty says that she's sticking with it because it's the best choice and she's too grateful to change her mind now. She wanted to do what was best for June Pope Weddings."

Sophie swallowed guilt. "I never said anything like that to her."

"Whatever the case, a bride should never feel like she has to choose what we think is best. In the best-case scenario, what she loves and what's best for her are one and the same. I tried to assure her that we would be more than happy to continue with the other dress, but she wouldn't change her mind. In any case, I put too much pressure on you to make this wedding worth the hoops we had to jump through to get it at the price you quoted. Let me take it from here."

With shaking hands, Sophie closed Ty's wedding binder and pushed it farther onto June's desk. She forced herself into a professional stance. She'd chosen the best dress possible for Ty; she knew it. And Ty would see the difference in the pictures of her and Anthony after the wedding, but Sophie wouldn't prove anything by throwing a tantrum in her mom's office.

"Now would be a good time to mention that I'll be taking some time to do a side job for Donavan Talbot." She rubbed her fingers along the outside of the binder. She wouldn't have time for Ty's wedding with the new stuff she needed to do for Donavan anyway.

June's eyes narrowed like David's had. Sophie clenched her jaw. "Like what?" June asked.

"He asked me to host a dating show and help him promote his business." She didn't want to stay any longer and discuss this with June, especially if it would resemble the "discussion" she'd had with David. Sophie tapped the binder. "Everything is up to date here. It should only take you a couple minutes to get up to speed with where we are on the Rogers-Daws wedding."

June flinched at the cool way Sophie referred to her friends' wedding, but Sophie didn't give her a chance to say anything else. Sophie marched out of the office to go find something else to work on.

For the rest of the morning, she kept herself busy and out of sight, even when Ty arrived. She ignored the way her heart dropped when David didn't follow her in, searching for Sophie, maybe to apologize. He was smart. If he couldn't support her in her dreams, it wouldn't work between them. That truth stood out to both of them.

An e-mail from Noah surprised David on Wednesday morning. His brother only wrote on P-days, Monday. *Transfers this week,* Noah started off. *We have P-day on Wednesday and I'm glad. Looks like you need some serious help, brother.* David chuckled at that. Typical Savage attitude: confident that he knew best. David had been guilty of it from time to time, maybe more often than not the last few weeks. *As for Jay, you've done what you can. I appreciate it. I know you won't give up, but don't worry too much. Someone Else has Jay in His hands. As for the girl? What do I know? I'm a missionary.*

David slapped his forehead, muttering good-naturedly, "Big help, Noah."

My suggestion? Noah went on. *Take a step back. And pray. Love, Elder Savage.*

Take a step back. Getting out of town did sound appealing. He could avoid Sophie pretty easily, no more tagging along on wedding-planning outings. And he could stay out of her way at the actual wedding. It and the reception would keep her as busy, if not busier, than she had been at the engagement party. He'd had to beg for her attention then.

He could walk away right now, though. He could forget the stupid way she'd left him empty. They hadn't even been that serious. That idea caught hold. Even if he got picked by a team in the draft that weekend, rookie training camp wouldn't start until mid-July. Of course, he could go to California and stay with his family until the wedding. But needing an out and having that in the form of baseball was like the sign he'd waited for. For the past six weeks, he'd gone back and forth.

Take a step back. Leave now.

Baseball.

Noah had advised him to pray, too, so David bowed his head. *I'm going to choose baseball. Does that sound good to You?* He waited, thinking about his love of baseball and how playing it every day had only increased that. He loved football too, but going back to baseball was natural.

Nothing amazing happened to answer his prayer, but David knew better than to expect that. He'd make the choice and take a step in the dark, see where it took him. The momentum behind his decision built, confirming his thoughts. He reached for his cell phone and dialed Clint Parry. By the time he hung up, Anthony and Ty had returned from a wedding-planning thing—flowers or something? He hadn't paid attention—and some of the knots in David's stomach had loosened. All he needed to do now was get himself to Lawrenceville, Georgia, as soon as he could and find out if he had the skills necessary to make the leap from not playing to Minor League.

"That sounded serious." Ty deposited several pizzas on the

coffee table. She grabbed a couple pieces and settled down in a chair next to the couch.

"It was pretty serious. Serious enough to get me to Georgia tomorrow." He waited. He should have discussed this some more with Anthony, given him a heads-up that they wouldn't be playing football with or against each other in the NFL for sure. But every time he brought it up, Anthony could only joke about it.

Ty scowled and leaned forward. "But ... what about you and Sophie? I thought things were getting serious with you two."

It surprised David that she brought Sophie up. Anthony had encouraged him to take the chance. Ty had wanted him to slow down.

"That's not an issue anymore."

Ty's gaze darted to Anthony in a panicked way. "I told you not to tell him about the dress thing—"

"No." David held his hands up. "It's about more. She's not who I thought she was."

Ty settled back in the chair and studied David. She shared another look with Anthony before saying, "You mean she's not who you wanted her to be."

He studied the floor. "Maybe." The unsettled churning he'd carried with him about Jay stretched out to include his judgments of Sophie. But her going to Donavan, selling that stupid website. Hadn't that made her choices more black and white too? He squeezed his eyes shut. No, he shouldn't judge Sophie for her decisions, as dumb as he considered them. But it always came back to him not being able to support her.

"That doesn't mean you should give up on her," Ty said.

David's head came up in surprise, then he shook it. "This isn't just about short skirts and wedding dresses."

Ty grabbed another slice of pizza. "Where are Sean and DJ?"

"Wait, wait, wait," Anthony jumped in. "You're not letting him off like that, are you?"

She reached up to lay a hand on his arm. "He's a big boy."

"Now is not the best time for him to make a decision about his future, his job, about football and baseball when he broke up with a girl and he's all emotional." Anthony moved behind Ty's chair and crossed his arms over his chest.

David snorted with laughter. "All emotional? Thanks, Dreamy."

"I'm serious. You need to sleep on this a couple nights." Anthony scowled.

David rubbed his hands together and forced himself to keep his gaze on Anthony. "I have. Lots of nights. Breaking up with Sophie made it easier to leave now."

Anthony gaped at him for several seconds without saying anything, his shoulders stiff. "So, seriously?"

"We've talked about this. You're getting married. Our lives are changing and moving on. Time for us to go our separate ways. You'll always be my first love. I cross my heart." David tried to keep a straight face as he injected some humor into the tense situation.

Ty, and finally Anthony, released a laugh. Wiping a fake tear away, Anthony pointed at David and then pounded his fist against his heart.

"Oh, stop it, you two. I'm getting jealous." Ty shook her head at them. "But what about the wedding?"

"I'll be back, I promise. But this feels like a good idea right now." And as he grabbed his pizza and settled back on the couch, the peace he'd asked for in his prayer settled over him. Was it because the distraction of Sophie had disappeared? Or because he'd made the right decision in going?

Thursday had ended up worse than Wednesday for Sophie. She'd tried to put on a happy face at work even though curling up in her bed and staying there for a few weeks sounded a lot easier. There was no need to break down over it. She'd split up with plenty of guys before. Just because she'd been friends with David for a long time and had fallen harder for him than any guy before him didn't mean she had to let this crush her.

And June kept popping in on Sophie's meetings that day and looking over her shoulder on any of the plans. Maybe Sophie imagined it, but it didn't matter. She felt useless and glad that she had other options. She'd never put a lot of thought into it before, but maybe she didn't belong at June Pope Weddings for the long term. Especially if her mom didn't trust her to do a good job.

When Sophie got home that evening, she kicked off her shoes at the door, dropped her bag, and flopped onto the couch. She turned on the TV to anything mind-numbing and settled in to avoid thinking for a while.

She snapped awake when Ally came in from work and shut the door. Sophie sat up and stared blearily at her roommate. Ally cast her a sympathetic look as she eyed the TV. Wait, sympathetic? Sophie had gotten through the last couple days without mentioning to Ally that her relationship with David had ended. How had she found out?

"*Project Runway?*" She pointed at the TV. "You hate that show. Saying goodbye to David at the airport must have sucked today."

"Airport?" Sophie repeated.

"I can imagine you're going to mope for a while, but can we watch something better than *Project Runway* reruns?" She picked up the remote and started flipping through channels.

As much as Sophie would rather forget about breaking up with David and not have a conversation with her best friend about him, she had to ask. "Where did David go?"

Ally paused, still holding the remote aloft, and shot Sophie a look of confusion. "To Georgia. To catch up with the Triple A team he'll be playing with." Ally put the remote down and faced Sophie. "He left without telling you?"

The same question had bounced around in Sophie's mind

since Ally'd mentioned him leaving. So he'd chosen baseball. She should have realized that would mean him leaving for the summer at least. When had he decided? Why hadn't he said anything?

So he was really done with her. Not even friends anymore. Not even back to the way it was before they dated. He would have at least sent a text then. That brought a lump to her throat.

The lump burned her chest when she swallowed it. Of course he was. Of course they couldn't go back. She'd said she was done and she meant that. She'd walked away from him. She'd *run* away from him. No friendship could recover from the things they'd said to each other.

But she wished he'd at least mentioned something to her. Even just a short message like *Chose baseball. Going to Georgia.*

Or *I'll miss you.* She sucked in a breath. Now she was really dreaming. But why did he have to just pick up and leave?

"Soph? Why didn't he tell you?"

Sophie emerged from her thoughts to find Ally watching her, concern drawing her eyebrows together and her mouth down into a frown.

"We broke up or whatever. So that's why."

"You guys broke up?" The concern opened up to shock. "What happened?"

"We're not a good match, end of story." Sophie burrowed farther into the blanket, hoping Ally would leave her alone, but of course her roommate would never allow Sophie to leave it at that.

She sat on the nearest open space on the couch and studied Sophie. "Why?"

"He freaked out over me helping Donavan promote his company, and I told David I was tired of trying to play dress-up for him and being some girl I'm not."

Several seconds went by before Ally responded. "So many things in that sentence to bang you over the head for, but let's go with the most disturbing. You're working for Donavan?"

Sophie dropped her head into the nearest pillow and

Sophie dropped her head into the nearest pillow and screamed. When she lifted her head, Ally regarded her calmly, unsurprised by the reaction. "Why does nobody see the awesome opportunity in this? Who cares about Donavan? He's giving me a chance to work on a show that will appear on a local TV station. Think about the experience! The name recognition I'll get. The things I could do with this! But no, the only thing anyone can do is rain on the stupid parade because he's behind it."

"Because he's toxic," Ally said. "Do you remember the year you dated him? I wasn't there for all of it, but you were a mess when we moved in together and seriously depressed before we did. Everyone breathed a collective sigh of relief when he called off the wedding and left you alone."

"But he's engaged. It's not like we're getting back together or anything." She gripped the edge of the pillow to keep her anger in check. Why couldn't she just get a congratulations on landing something so cool?

"He. Is. Toxic." Ally clenched her own jaw. "I hate the fact that you'll be close enough for him to spread his ugliness to you. Don't do it, Soph. Don't let him back in at all, because he will figure out a way to put you under his thumb. It's not worth fifteen minutes of fame."

"This is not about getting famous," Sophie shot back. "Are you not listening?"

"You're not thinking about it logically, Soph. I know how Donavan works. You're his pretty face. That's what this job will do for you."

"You're wrong." Sophie shook her head. She wouldn't let Ally's prejudice against Donavan ruin her chance at her dream. Hosting a reality show, being a part of the PR.

"And David's wrong too?" Ally challenged.

"He doesn't like Donavan's company and said something about how I was willing to lower my standards for the chance to get on TV. All he cares about is that I'm not the perfect girl he thought he could make me."

"What are you selling for Donavan?" If anything, Ally's eyes narrowed further. Sophie couldn't blame the instant distrust, but couldn't Ally give her a chance to show her it wasn't as bad as she made it sound?

"I'm not selling anything. I'm hosting a mini-dating show to promote his website, Mormon Mixer. It's a combination dating and social media site."

Ally snorted. "Well, I can't agree on Donavan giving anyone advice on dating. What's his take?"

Sophie only hesitated a moment. "It's about setting up beautiful people with other beautiful people."

Ally rolled her eyes.

"But I'm not following him into a life of sin. That's what David made it sound like."

"It sounds elitist, which isn't surprising."

"It's just a job. And it sounds like I'd be good at it. It could be a stepping stone. I've already got all these ideas about how to take it a step further, how to make it better. I'm not the girl I was before. I can stand up to him this time."

Ally studied her for a few seconds. "You should call David and talk to him. Maybe if he understood more about it ... Don't write him off so quick, Sophie. He's a good guy, and he made you happy."

Sophie shook her head. "I'm not going to change who I am for another guy. You're the one who went on and on about how terrible Donavan was for me."

"Because Donavan is evil. He brings you down. He's critical and soul-sucking."

"And David is judgmental. What's the difference?"

Falling back onto the couch, Ally reached her hands toward the ceiling. "You are so stubborn sometimes." She dropped her hands and sat back up, ignoring Sophie's *dramatic-much?* expression at her theatrics. "When are you going to get it? You are not an object, Sophie. You're a woman. A smart, confident woman who doesn't need Donavan in order to take over the world."

"I know that."

"Well, that's not what you're telling people if you're selling beauty over substance."

"My confidence doesn't revolve around what people think."

"What you represent says it does. Doing this show will say that looks and admiration are important. Not your mind. Not your abilities. You'll be bending to what people want. What Donavan wants."

"That's not fair." The burn in Sophie's chest had spread as her roommate attacked. She acted like Sophie walked around staring at herself in mirrors. "How come when a woman cares about clothes and fashion, she's vain and shallow? Maybe I just need a different hobby, right? If I wanted to find a cure for cancer and Donavan could pay for the research, we wouldn't be having this conversation, would we? I just have the wrong dreams."

"That's not what I'm saying, Sophie. David and I know that you don't need Donavan to get a show on a local TV station or gather up some big-time clients if you want to do PR. Or to find a cure for cancer, for that matter. Don't be so surprised when the people who love you want to protect you from someone we know will hurt you."

Sophie dropped her head back against the couch. She didn't want to hear Ally's logic. Maybe she could get all that stuff on her own, but it could take her years. Why was it so bad to take what she could now when it was right in front of her? Sophie understood that they were worried about her throwing her lot in with Donavan, but it wasn't like they were getting back together. This was purely a business relationship. Sophie could handle herself.

But nobody else seemed to believe that.

She stood up, all of Ally's words building inside her, her frustration growing with every second she thought about it. "Forgive me if I don't take relationship advice from you, Ally," she snapped, knowing the words were mean and unfair but wanting to strike back anyway. Besides, Ally hadn't had a serious boyfriend since before Sophie had met her. What did she know?

Ally stood quickly, her hands on her hips, tears shimmering in her eyes, and glared at Sophie. "Don't be stupid. Don't let David go over a misunderstanding like this. Trust me on this. And don't go back to Donavan, no matter how you do it." She stomped away, toward the stairs.

Real, horrible guilt flooded over Sophie immediately for saying what she had. "Ally?" But her roommate had already disappeared. Sophie slumped back down and buried her face in the pillow again. Even if Ally was right about David understanding once they talked about the thing with Donavan, even if she was right about Donavan, David had already hopped a plane bound for Georgia. And he hadn't bothered to tell her.

chapter eighteen

SOPHIE PULLED into a spot right in front of the club where she'd agreed to meet Donavan and his crew and managed a smile. First sign of good luck all week. If tonight went well, she could prove to everyone how wrong they'd been about this opportunity. She checked her purse for the list of ideas to talk over with Donavan or his partner after they taped tonight. She could agree with everyone on at least one thing—she wasn't going to stay with Donavan, even as an employee, for long. She had bigger plans than that. Proving herself tonight, to Donavan, his partner, the TV station, whoever, was only the beginning.

And she looked good. Nailing this outfit would prove her superb fashion know-how. She went for professional but hip. Date night one-upped. Black straight-leg jeans, a loose, teal blouse, a light grey blazer, chunky bracelets, and a simple gold necklace.

All of it. Perfect.

She stepped out of her car onto the sidewalk. She loved the ambience of the streetlights glowing and the music filtering out of the club. Not a bad facade, she thought as she started toward it.

"Sophie! Glad you're early." Donavan strode through the front door to meet her and held out a hand away from the building. "This way. We have a trailer parked in the parking garage over here that you can use for a dressing room."

"I don't need one, just a place to stash my purse." Sophie stepped away from him. Ally's words about Donavan spreading his attitude on her washed into her brain like a giant wave the minute she saw him.

Donavan scrutinized her before gazing upward and shaking his head. "You need the dressing room, Soph. You're not wearing that on air."

She folded her arms. She hated admitting Ally might have been right, but at least she wasn't second-guessing herself like she would have two years ago. "I look fine. More than fine. Great."

"Sure, if you're planning on dating some guy with no taste. It's my company you're representing. You need to show our image." He waved over a woman, the blonde Sophie had seen him with at the cake shop. "Cam has clothes for you."

The woman bounced forward, shifting the clothes to one arm and shoving her other hand out, so eager to please that Sophie couldn't bring herself to say anything more. She pressed her lips together and forced a pleasant expression.

"Hi, I'm Cam. You must be Sophie." She beamed, her face glowing with approval. "We brought some clothes in case you weren't sure what to wear, but you look awesome so—"

"She needs to change. Now," Donavan snapped. Red swept up the woman's cheeks, but he ignored it. "And you two need to hurry. The guy and girl we're filming are already here, waiting in their cars, and we want Sophie there for their first meeting." Donavan pivoted away, dismissing them both.

"The trailer is this way." Cam hurried on ahead, not giving Sophie a chance to comfort her in any way. How had a nice woman like her gotten sucked in with someone like Donavan?

Well, her looks. She had long, wispy blonde hair and diamond-clear blue eyes. Watching the way her hair swayed as she walked brought to mind her picture on Donavan's cards: blue eyes popping and blonde hair blowing across her face. Model quality, for sure.

"I saw your picture on Donavan's cards." Sophie hurried to catch up as they entered the parking garage. "They're gorgeous."

"Thanks. Donavan knows a photographer who can work magic." Cam grimaced and pointed to a white, enclosed trailer. "That's us. We better hurry."

Sophie swallowed the angry words burning her throat. In time Donavan would destroy this woman—despite her obvious beauty, he'd leave her shattered and under the impression she couldn't live her life right without him. This woman should turn tail and run now. But who was Sophie to talk? She was here, wasn't she?

"Here you go." Cam showed her inside the trailer, where a section had been partitioned off. Cam pushed the curtain aside and laid the clothes over a clothing rack. Sophie wondered if Donavan had made anyone else change. "Better hurry." Cam smiled weakly and pulled the curtain shut behind her.

Sophie scrutinized the outfit. A mustard-colored skirt belted at the waist lay on top. Okay, not too bad. She shimmied out of her jeans, tossed aside her shirt, and kicked off her heels.

The skirt hit mid-thigh. Sophie twisted around, double-checking the size, but Donavan had gotten it right. She took a deep breath and grabbed the shirt, a loose, black-and-white striped tank top. She slipped it on, then tucked it in and pulled out a little to let it drape. It wasn't too revealing, with wide straps and a pretty high scoop-neck.

Stop it. She glared at herself in the mirror and then whirled away, grabbing the black, high-heeled booties and slipping them on before pushing aside the curtain. She would have never thought twice about this outfit before dating David, and since she was done pleasing him, she didn't need to think twice about it now. She looked great. Sure, it wasn't the polished, hip image she'd meant to have, but she'd overlook that for now. Once she blew everyone away on the show, she'd make Donavan let her have more say in her wardrobe.

"Wow," Cam said when Sophie walked out. "Donavan's right. You're perfect for this."

"Thanks." But as Sophie followed, her confidence started to shake. David's stupid words about how her clothes made her feel kept pounding against her brain with every step she took out of the parking garage, down the sidewalk, and back toward the club. Did she feel strong and confident?

Why shouldn't she? It was a fun outfit. Something she might have picked out for herself. But ... did she?

She pinched her lips together. Honestly? Not really. Donavan had her on display. Like he had every time she went out with him while they were dating—the pretty face. For looks only.

Donavan glanced up from a conversation with a camera guy as they approached. His trademark slow-appreciative smile spread over his lips. "Good. You're finally here. Much better."

That did it. Sophie froze three feet short of him and shook her head. "No way. I'm not doing this thing in this skirt."

Donavan reached out for her arm and tried pulling her forward. She yanked away and glared at him. Scowling, Donavan said, "Listen, Sophie. You work for me. You're doing this to help my company, and this is my company's image."

Sophie waved her hand over the clothes. "This outfit says that I care more about how I look and what people think than anything else. It does not say professional. It does not say 'has it all together.' It says party girl, and that is *not* who I am." She shook her head, angry at repeating Ally's words, but angrier that she had even changed in the first place. "But that's what your website is all about, isn't it? Pretty girls. Pretty guys. Who cares that they're all about as deep as a kiddie pool."

Donavan's face reddened. "The website is about showing people that Mormon singles aren't all a bunch of people who sit around at lame dances drinking punch, trying to get married and pop out babies as fast as they can. It's about showing people that we can be hip and edgy too."

"Edgy?" Sophie quirked an eyebrow. "Listen, I film in the outfit I came here in, or I don't do it at all."

"I'm calling the shots here. I hired you. You do what I say. You look way better in this than whatever you had on earlier—it looked like you got it out of your mom's closet." He folded his arms across his chest, pressing his lips together. His expression said he meant to end the argument and believed he had the better opinion. Too many times that had worked in the past. Not today.

She folded her own arms and laughed at him. Laughed at herself for being so taken in. She'd let the appeal of a TV show and the possibilities blind her to the fact that David, her mom, and Ally had all been right. She'd wondered why they expected her to climb up the mountain the hard way when the easy, smooth trail was right in front of her. She didn't see that there was something to be said for conquering the mountain.

"Why did I *ever* let you back into my head? I have always known better than you what looks good on me. My mom has brides coming into her shop because I can choose killer gowns for them. The girls at the Dream Dress Project beg Corinne to let me pick out their dresses. And you think that I'm going to bow down and let *you* tell me what looks good on me?" She pressed a finger into his chest, backing him away from her. "No. Way." She whirled on the heels and marched back toward the parking garage, meeting a stunned Cam about three steps away.

On a roll already, Sophie couldn't keep her words to herself. "A piece of advice, Cam. You're gorgeous and sweet, but if you stay with him much longer, he'll suck it all out of you. I can already see it in your eyes. Run while you still can."

After a record-breaking change of three minutes, Sophie strode out of the parking garage without looking back. Despite a few bumps, she was a fabulous wedding planner. She loved that. If getting a spot on TV would take a few more years of hard work, so be it, if that's what she still wanted. She could pitch her ideas to someone herself. She bet if she thought about it hard enough, June Pope Weddings probably already had someone on file she could talk to. She should have listened to David right off. Researched Donavan's company more. Believed in herself more. She hadn't realized how comfortable she'd been with the changes she'd made in herself until she'd worn something that put her on display. And then hated it. How had she ever expected to have a real relationship when her need to please took up all the attention? Without all that, she and David got hamburgers together and talked. About everything. About peanut butter and jelly and Donavan and her goals. About how she loved clothes—not how good they looked on her, but the art she saw in them. David understood her the way she'd hoped for two years that Anthony would. The way she'd thought Donavan had.

"Sophie! Wait!"

She turned to see Cam waving at her from the sidewalk. She paused but held her hand up. "You're not going to talk me into going back in there, even if he lets me wear this," Sophie said.

"No. I'm just wondering if you'll give me a ride." Cam folded her arms in front of her and rocked forward, newfound freedom evident in her buoyant movements, the light in her eyes brighter than even a few moments before.

As Sophie put her arm around Cam's elbow, she felt the lightness in her own steps. "I have a feeling we're going to be great friends."

When Sophie got back to her apartment, Ally sat on the couch reading a book. Her roommate, who'd been on "polite" terms with her since their argument the night before, raised her eyebrows. "How'd things go?"

Sophie tossed her purse to the side and plopped down next to Ally, surprising her by laying her tired head on Ally's shoulder.

"It didn't go." Sophie closed her eyes. "You were right. You were so right. Donavan put me in a short skirt to 'better represent' the website. After a brief lapse, I told him to shove it and walked out. It felt *good*."

Ally pulled away, but when Sophie straightened and looked up at her, her roommate was smiling. "You told him off?"

"I really gave it to him, and I still came up with a bunch of stuff on the way home that I should have said." Sophie let out a big sigh. "It hit me, standing there in that skirt, which was actually cute, that I didn't feel like me at all. Pretty would be the only thing people would ever see in me if I stuck with Donavan's show. I wasn't a smart executive. I wasn't about to blow anyone away with my ideas. I bowed to Donavan's will all over again, pretending like next time would be better. I went on and on to you and my mom and David about how I went there to get PR experience, but I looked like someone on spring break."

Ally tapped on Sophie's forehead. "Glad you finally got it."

"Because of you." She rested her head against the back of the couch to face Ally. "What happened, Al?"

Ally shook her head to herself and took a deep breath. "A little while before I met you I was dating this guy seriously. Russell. He was fantastic, better than even David." Her eyes gleamed as she spoke of him, from the slight wetness collecting there or maybe the leftover feelings—Sophie couldn't decide. "I was barely twenty and so in love, and I didn't think twice about anything with him. I started wearing shorter skirts, or dresses, and smaller shirts or whatever because I wanted him to think I was pretty." She paused and gazed into space for several minutes before going on. "Anyway, things went too far one night, and I freaked. I broke up with him and blamed everything on how I'd changed myself. I never stopped to consider that I encouraged him to kiss me, to touch me and ... whatever. And I'm not saying it was all the clothes I wore or anything, but I felt different in them. Sexier. Bolder. You know? I don't want to preach to you, Soph. I don't. So much of that whole thing was because Russell and I both got too comfortable with each other and took tiny steps down the path we ended up on."

Sophie reached an arm around her shoulders and pulled Ally close. "I understand. I figured it out this morning that I quit being such a snob around David when I wore different things. Less fashionista and more fun. I didn't realize how much I liked it until he left."

Ally pulled away. "So call him. Tell him that."

Sophie shook her head. "No. He's gone ... and if he'd wanted to work things out he would have called by now. Or told me he was leaving. Or something. We both dove into this without realizing how it would change our friendship—and it's too late to go back to that."

Groaning, Ally tapped her head again. "You have watched way too many romantic comedies." But she left it at that. "Come on," she said, grabbing Sophie's hand. "Let's go out for dinner."

Sophie looked down at her clothes. "But not in this outfit. Tonight, I'm going to need something a lot looser."

chapter nineteen

DAVID STEPPED off the plane in Salt Lake City and looked out the windows. He could drive to Provo right now and knock on Sophie's door. He'd be kidding himself if he tried to pretend like it was the first time he'd thought of her after three weeks on the road with the Gwinnett Braves, the Atlanta Braves' affiliate Triple A team. When he'd busted out of Provo at the end of May, he'd figured he'd spend all his time on baseball and none of it on missing Sophie Pope. And in truth, during games and practices he didn't have much time to think about her. But travel time and nights in hotels and any time baseball didn't distract him, his mind went to one place, even when he told himself he hadn't been serious enough about her for her to invade his thoughts like this, to miss her as much as he did, to want to forget all the realities and just beg her to give him another chance.

More than once he'd picked up his phone to call and apologize for not supporting her with the job Donavan had offered. David understood the draw for her. Sure, she found the perfect dresses for every bride and knew all the places to call for a top-notch wedding reception, but she wanted her dream. Hadn't he done the same thing by choosing baseball over football?

Then he'd remember the website and the way Donavan had talked to his fiancée in the cake shop and why David couldn't understand her choice in the first place. How could he apologize for not supporting her when he still couldn't support her? When the thought of Donavan getting any piece of her again made him crazy?

Now he was back in Utah. She was so close, and Ty's advice, *that doesn't mean you should give up on her,* kept bringing him back around.

"David!"

He glanced up. He'd made it all the way from the gate without paying attention at all. Ty and Anthony waited for him near the luggage carousel. Since he could stay only until Wednesday night after the reception, he'd brought a carry-on. They could skip waiting for luggage.

"Hey." He quickened his step and met them. "You guys ready to do this thing?"

Anthony squeezed Ty's hand. "You mean this wedding thing's not over yet? Seems like we've done so much already..."

Ty ignored him. "How's baseball?"

"Awesome. Ready for training camp?" He followed them toward the doors.

"Stoked for it. Can't wait to get to the good stuff again."

By the time they reached the car, they'd gotten the sports talk out of the way, and Ty asked the question he figured she'd waited through their conversation to ask. "Have you talked to Sophie at all?"

"No." David tossed his bag into the back of Anthony's car and got in behind the driver's seat. "You think I should have?" he asked sarcastically.

Ty got in and shifted in her seat to face him. "I told you not to give up on her. You obviously didn't listen."

He studied his hands. "I've thought about her a lot. More than I figured I would after I left. I'll admit it—she's a big part of the reason I skipped town."

"So I was right. You shouldn't have given up on her," Ty said.

David met Anthony's eye in the rearview mirror and chuckled. "No gloating," David said.

"Why did you break up with her?" Ty pressed.

"I didn't. She broke up with me."

"If you want to get technical. Why'd you let her do it?" She settled back against the window, facing Anthony and half-turned toward David.

Ty wouldn't give up until David gave her an answer, so he figured he might as well cave. Anthony wouldn't be any help in fending her off, and David could use her advice. He still took a moment to compose his thoughts and figure out how to best put this to her. She might be cheering for Sophie right now, but David didn't want her old reservations to come up. "Sophie's ex, Donavan, that creep we met in the cake shop? He offered her a job to host a dating show to promote his website."

"What kind of website?"

"That's the thing. It's a social media site for 'hot Mormons.' It says that right on its front page. I couldn't agree with her lowering herself just to get experience in PR."

Ty didn't answer for a long time. So long that David bent forward and shared a look with Anthony, who shrugged but kept his mouth shut.

"Nobody's perfect," she said.

"I know that."

She leaned over the center console to talk to him. "Do you? Because every time you take a woman out, it's like you expect her to measure up to all these things you want in a relationship right away. And if she doesn't, no big deal because there'll be another woman for you to evaluate."

"I'm not … it's not like that." But he'd heard it so much from Jay, Sophie, and now Ty, he couldn't deny it. He'd started out telling himself that Sophie needed a real friend, an example of how good men treated women, but he'd expected to change her. And when that didn't work, he bailed. Wasn't that exactly what he'd done?

"David, you can't make her fit your mold of perfection. If you don't want to work at it with her, that's fine. You probably will find someone else, and maybe that someone else will fit the mold better than she did. But if you're thinking about her this much, maybe it's time to reevaluate your mold."

David didn't like the way this conversation brought back all the reasons he'd found to bypass girls. The way he'd disregarded Katie because she'd fawned over Ty's ring and how he'd thought of her as high-maintenance when she'd asked for a different drink.

"Maybe," he mumbled. He let the freeway capture his attention as they drove to Provo. He and Anthony had dated their fair share of girls and then some, but David had wanted a serious relationship, to find a woman and settle down. When Anthony had met Ty, David redoubled his efforts to find the right woman. He hadn't wanted Anthony leaving him behind, getting what David wanted when Anthony wasn't even trying.

Ty didn't push him anymore. She and Anthony started talking, leaving him to his thoughts. He shut his eyes against the barrage of reasons he'd found to pass on all the women Ty had introduced him to in the last six months. She was right. He had his idea of what a perfect woman should be. His mom had taught him to treat women like queens—but maybe he'd executed that the wrong way. Expected them to be queens all the time, to be perfect, to deserve the pedestal he set them on. It shouldn't surprise him that none had measured up to the bar he set. And yeah, he'd almost prided himself on the knowledge that he was desired enough that there'd always be another woman to date so it didn't matter that he judged them all as too high-maintenance or that they didn't like sports enough. Sometime, somewhere, there'd be a different woman who was perfect for him.

Maybe he'd even thought that with Sophie. That after her he'd find another woman he could have that much fun with, but wouldn't be ... Sophie. And he had fallen in love with Sophie. Not just the woman he took care of the night she was sick, not just the woman who ate hamburgers with him at Red Robin and experimented with ramen noodles. He also loved the one who pulled herself together with class when Ciara Kelley had shoved past wrongs in her face, but who trusted David with the truth about who she'd been. The woman who, for better or worse, knew exactly what Donavan's offer could do for her career, for her dreams. The woman who had the strength to defy the people she cared about to take that chance.

He loved everything about that woman. He just couldn't stand by her, as badly as he wanted to.

As they walked into the house, David's cell phone rang. He hoped, despite it all, to see Sophie's number on the caller ID. To his surprise, it was Jay's.

"Hey? You have great timing. I just got in to town." David dropped his bag on the couch.

Ty nudged him. "Sophie?" she mouthed. He shook his head and turned away from her disappointed half-frown. Disappointed? What a turnaround.

"For real, dude? That's great," Jay said. David didn't mistake the relief in Jay's voice.

"What's up?"

"I hoped you were around. Anthony's getting married this week, right? I didn't want to have to call my mom..."

David furrowed his brow. "What's going on, Jay?"

"There was an accident ... and I'm fine, but I've been arrested, and I need you to come and get me."

Jay had reassured David a few times that he was fine, despite the accident, despite the alcohol involved. He just needed someone to come pick him up and take him home. And smack him over the head, in David's opinion. That didn't keep him from worrying or from running his finger over his mom's number a few times. He might need her to give him Jay's mom's phone number. He'd find out how serious it was first.

Jay met him in the lobby and stood as soon as David entered, walking toward him briskly.

"Thanks for coming."

"Have you talked to your mom yet?" David asked, letting Jay lead the way back out of the station house. He couldn't blame the kid for wanting to get out fast.

Jay shook his head and waved at him. "I'm not a kid, David."

David caught the way Jay's voice shook, maybe with fear, but he couldn't let this slide. He'd backed off. He'd tried to stay in touch by texting every once in a while. But he couldn't hang in the background after this.

He grabbed Jay's arm and spun him around to face him. Jay tried to yank away, but David held firm. "Why am I here, Jay? Why'd you call me? You have plenty of friends who could drive down here and pick you up, so why me?"

Jay folded his arms and stared at the black sky before taking a deep breath. "I don't know. It just felt right to call you, and for the first time in a while, I listened to what felt right." He sighed, his shoulders slumping.

David nodded and studied Jay, relief trickling through him. So maybe ... maybe he hadn't been that bad of a friend to Jay. Maybe he'd done something right if in the moment Jay needed someone, even for something as small as a ride—even if he didn't realize himself what else he might need tonight—he'd called David. It didn't make everything okay. It didn't mean Jay was going to wake up the next morning and start filling out his mission papers, but it meant something.

"What happened tonight?" David asked, gently.

Jay shook his head, but it looked more like remorse than denial. "My roommate Caleb and I were out, yeah ... you know."

"Partying? Drinking?"

"Sure." Jay shoved his hands into his pockets. "We were driving home, and Caleb hit a pole. Nobody got hurt, we're both fine, but ..." Jay blew out another breath and studied the sidewalk.

"You were both drunk."

"Yeah. I'm gonna get this huge fine for underage drinking, but it's nothing compared to Caleb, dude." He met David's eyes. "He's messed. Underage DUI and all that. We've both got court dates, but he might get jail time and pretty much the works." He paused for several seconds before going on. "Well, when are you going to say it?"

"Say what?" David asked. Jay looked shaken up, and truth was, the story shook David up too. As bad as Jay thought the situation was for his friend Caleb, it could have ended up a lot worse if they'd hit someone else. Maybe David didn't need to tell Maggie, if only to save her from a heart attack at how close Jay had come to what could have been a tragedy.

"'I told you so.' I've pretty much been waiting for you to bust that out since I called you."

"You could be dead, Jay. 'I told you so' and me asking if you're going to play baseball again are the least of your worries."

Jay's gaze turned back to the sidewalk. "Yeah."

David laid a hand on his shoulder and pulled him into a one-armed headlock-slash-hug. "I'm going to drive you home now. You can figure out what you're going to tell your mom, and I can get some sleep. According to the wedding itinerary Ty showed me, there's a lot going on in the next couple days." He started toward his car.

"Thanks, David," Jay said quietly.

"No problem." Would this be enough to wake Jay up about his choices? David hoped so. He'd hate for Jay to have to learn a much tougher lesson.

chapter twenty

SOPHIE HAD DONE everything that morning to keep herself busy and her mind off the fact that David was in town, at his house with Anthony, putting on his tux ... She stopped herself before she pictured him in the tux. If he'd wanted to talk to her after the immature way she'd treated him, he would have called or texted or something in the last few weeks. He hadn't.

"Sophie?" Kaylie tapped on the office door and leaned in. "The delivery guy from Silhouettes dropped this off." She held out a white garment bag.

"We weren't expecting anything from them, were we?" Sophie stood and crossed the room to take the bag. In order to keep David off her mind, she'd found every possible detail to attend to at the office—tying up every loose end, going over all the active weddings for anything they might have missed. She'd kept track of everything going on. As she took the hanger from Kaylie, the index card the wedding dress shop used to identify the recipients caught Sophie's eye. "TyAnne Daws," followed by today's date—her wedding day.

Sophie's frown fell into a full scowl. "We cancelled this order weeks ago." She hung the dress on the nearby coatrack and unzipped the garment bag halfway to confirm what she suspected. Yep. Ty's Grecian dress. Sophie shook her head. She'd cancelled the order herself, so Ty couldn't change her mind again. How had this happened?

As she opened the garment bag further, she found a note pinned to the bag. "June, we'd already started rush alterations on this dress after your bride's fitting in order to make the timeline. We're not going to be able to sell it. Maybe your bride can take some pretty pictures in it for us? I'm sure you can find someone else who loves it too. Best, Angela."

"Hmmmm." Sophie thought back to the pictures they'd taken at Ty's fitting. She *had* glowed with happiness. Sophie let her fingers trail over the soft fabric on the bodice and over the dropped waist that had caused so many problems. Well—that Sophie had caused so many problems over.

She was right that this dress wasn't for Ty, but David was right too. Ty should wear this dress. Contract or whatever, it was her wedding day and time for Sophie to swallow her pride.

She checked her watch. Only fifteen minutes until Ty was supposed to be inside the temple. That would cut it close. Sophie didn't think twice. She zipped the bag back up, grabbed it, and raced out of the office.

"Where are you going?" Kaylie asked when Sophie reached the door—and realized she'd forgotten her purse.

"Taking this to Ty," Sophie called as she doubled back to the office.

"That's not the dress she's wearing," Kaylie said when Sophie returned.

"Yes, it is." Sophie shoved the door open and took the stairs two at a time. She clamped her mouth shut to keep from swearing when she hit her sixth red light between the office and the temple. Well, if she didn't make it, she didn't make it, but she'd try her hardest to get this dress to Ty.

When she pulled into the parking lot at the temple, she spotted a group of people heading inside the doors. Sophie pulled into the first spot available and sprinted. Sure enough, Ty, her mom, June, and Anthony strolled down the sidewalk, Ty and

Anthony holding hands and chatting as they followed June and Ty's mom.

"Ty! Ty!" Sophie shouted. The group paused, and even from as far away as she was, Sophie saw the scowl on June's face.

"What's going on, Sophie?" June asked, opening the door of the temple. "Ty is supposed to be inside right now."

"*Silhouettes* delivered this dress this morning. It's already altered. Ty should wear it." Sophie angled away from her mom, who held the garment bag for the Jovi Roy dress that Sophie had insisted Ty wear, and addressed Ty. "You love it a lot more."

Guilty delight turned Ty's lips, and she eyed the garment bag longingly. "No. You were right about that dress. And besides, we had an agreement with you."

Sophie shook her head as soon as Ty said no. "I am right about this dress, but I had an agreement with you to give you your dream wedding no matter what. You love this dress. You should be wearing it."

Ty glanced at Sophie then June. June gave Ty a small nod. "I ... don't know," Ty said.

"Why don't you wear both?" Ty's mom broke in. "They're both already altered. We have them both. Can she wear one to get married in and take pictures here and then the other one at the reception?"

Ty's face lit up. "Can I?"

"Great idea." June's nod picked up speed. "But we do need to get inside now."

Ty took the garment bag from Sophie. "Thanks, Sophie."

"I'm sorry about the way I treated you, Ty. I really am."

"It's okay." Ty reached over with her free arm and hugged Sophie.

"We'll see you later?"

"Sure." Sophie peered at June. "If I'm still invited."

"You did too much not to be." Ty waved as Anthony took the garment bag.

"We won't be the only ones looking for you." He winked and followed the others inside.

Sophie froze on the sidewalk. Did he mean that David wanted to see her? But if that was true, why hadn't he tried to contact her after he'd left?

She headed back to her car, her thoughts on David as she drove to the office, until she passed Eufloria. On a whim, she pulled in. She already had one apology under her belt. She might as well get another in. Anything to keep her mind off seeing David and not making up with him.

As she headed for the entrance, she had to take a couple deep breaths. More likely than not, Ciara would reject her before she even got the words out. But Sophie wanted this off her chest once and for all. As long as she could get out "I'm sorry," she'd done her part.

It was her lucky day. Ciara was stocking some plants right near the entrance. Sophie could make a quick getaway if things went south.

"Hi, Ciara," she said to get her attention.

Ciara looked up, scowled, and then stood, dusting off her black trousers. "I'll get someone to help you."

"I'm here to talk to you." Sophie clenched her hands together and took a deep breath, waiting for the words to come to her. To her surprise, fear flitted across Ciara's face before she covered it with a deep slant of her eyebrows.

"About what?"

"High school. You probably don't believe this, but I've regretted ruining your dress since I did it. I'm sorry. Can I do something to make it up to you?" Sophie watched as Ciara's expression shifted from anger to skepticism to confusion.

"How can you make up for ruining my prom?"

Sophie resisted the urge to point out that Preston had played a big part. But getting into an argument with Ciara wouldn't be a very good apology. "I work with my mom who's a wedding planner, one of the best in Utah. Are you married?"

Ciara's confusion increased. "No."

"Okay, well when you do get married, you can call us." Sophie dug a card out of her purse and handed it over. "I can get you a dress—whatever you want—and I'll do it for free."

Ciara squinted at the card. Then she met Sophie's eye again. "Is it true that you work with the Dream Dress Project I saw on the news a while ago?"

Sophie blinked. "Yeah. How did you know?"

"That guy you were with came back later that day and told me about it. I didn't believe him. That doesn't sound like you."

Sophie's heart soared at the thought of David sticking up for her like that. "I did it to try and make up for what I did to you, but I love it so much I don't know if it's much good as penance." Sophie's shoulders relaxed. Ciara had accepted her apology. That was all Sophie needed.

Until her scowl returned. "Why didn't you just tell me you were sorry then?"

Sophie burst into laughter. "I was eighteen and a brat. It's been five years, and I've changed—a little."

Ciara waved the card. "I'll think about this. I mean, it's a long way off since I don't have a boyfriend or anything, but ... well, thanks."

Sophie and Ciara would never be friends, she could tell that. Even if Ciara had accepted the apology, the tightness in her jaw and lips said she still remembered too much of Sophie's mean-girl act in high school for anything more than them being able to work together when Sophie had business with Eufloria.

"No problem," Sophie said instead of trying to continue an awkward conversation. She left the store, her arms swinging and peace warming her. When she got back to her car, she leaned her head against the headrest. And smiled. Amazing how those two conversations could lift so much weight off her chest.

Now she needed to figure out this thing with David. So he had gone back and defended her. It shouldn't surprise Sophie. It was so him. She'd first started to give him her heart the day he rescued her at the cake shop, and he had kept on charging in on his white horse to defend her. Tears stung at Sophie's eyes, and she chided herself. It was over. She'd had three weeks to work through this.

But he was such a great guy, and his actions had always shown it. How could she work through losing him? How could she give him up?

She couldn't. She just *couldn't*.

Sophie had spent plenty of time in her room over the years, agonizing over the clothes in her closet, trying to decide on the perfect outfit, but nothing compared to the difficulty of dressing for Anthony and Ty's reception. She had a good pick of gorgeous yet I'm-in-the-background–type dresses for all the weddings she'd helped her mom with, but that wouldn't work tonight. Not to impress David and figure out if he'd written her off forever or if they still had a chance.

After changing far too many times for her own good, she settled on a shimmery gray dress with a lace overlay, belted at the waist. Cap sleeves. Elegant and killer at the same time.

June kept her busy every minute leading up to the arrival of the new Mr. and Mrs. Rogers. Sophie rested against the doorway separating the magical garden setting Ty had chosen for the reception from the messiness that happened behind the scenes. She sighed when Ty floated in at Anthony's side—no one would notice that she might look shorter in that dress. Ty had been right about one thing: it was the perfect dress for her.

Months ago, Sophie had expected this moment would devastate her. But her grin kept stretching until it threatened to slip off the sides of her cheeks. She clapped enthusiastically with the rest of the crowd, and when she took her eyes off the blissful couple taking the dance floor, she caught David's attention.

He looked—amazing. Tanned, no doubt from all the time in

the sun, chasing baseballs around center field. She'd listened to his games and looked up his stats online. He played great, of course. Wowed everyone with how he'd adjusted to playing baseball again. He looked happy. He even smiled when he held her gaze for longer than a chance glimpse. But he didn't move in her direction. After a moment, a too-short moment, he turned back to Anthony and Ty and wolf-whistled.

Sophie shrank back against the doorway. There. That was her answer, right? In every movie she'd ever seen, every book she'd read with a hint of romance—after that look the hero came bounding over and swept the woman into his arms. David was that type of guy. He'd been her hero. But he hadn't moved toward her at all. Not even leaned.

She straightened. What had he called her when they'd first started dating? A force. Strong. Confident. She didn't have to shrink away because the guy she loved didn't love her back.

She didn't have to stand there, waiting for him.

Chucking her pity over her shoulder, she strode out into the room toward him. He caught her eye in time to watch her take the last few steps, and fear might have flashed across his expression. Good.

Part of David figured it'd be a good idea to get out right now because a couple seconds under Sophie's spell would have him right back where he shouldn't be. Loving her and knowing they couldn't make it work. The other part didn't move. Of course he couldn't. She strode across the room with her shoulders square, not a bit down and out about not seeing him for three weeks. Sophie wouldn't, though. She'd probably gotten a lot of success under her belt since he'd left. Enough to take her mind off him. He'd tried to find the videos or clips of her show and couldn't. It hadn't helped that she never told him what station to look on.

So he just stood there and said, "Hey," when she reached him.

"Hey." She took a deep breath and clasped her hands in front of her. "So, listen, there's something I need to tell you."

He put his hands in his pockets and rocked back on his heels. He needed to distance himself from her, even if only a few inches. Already the pull to put his arm around her and take her out onto the dance floor threatened to win out over common sense. What could it hurt? He'd be gone again in the morning anyway.

"Oh, yeah?"

She kept her gaze on his face. "You were right. Absolutely right. I walked out before we even started shooting, but it shouldn't have taken me that long."

Lightning shot through David. His mouth might have dropped open as he stared at her. Could it be this easy? All along, the only thing holding him back was Sophie's decision to back Donavan, and she hadn't done it.

She kept talking. "I thought you wanted to change me or something, like how Donavan always told me to dress and act a certain way. I can't believe I ever compared you to a jerk like him. It took a couple smacks to the head from Ally, but I get it all now, and I'm sorry. I'm sorry I ruined everything by acting so immature."

David laughed. It was too hard to believe that he could really have what he wanted. He could have Sophie—the real Sophie, the whole Sophie. He grabbed her and pulled her into his arms, burying his face against her neck. He thought he'd left the weight of his ruined relationship in Provo when he'd gone off to play baseball, but he didn't understand how much he'd truly needed her until the weight lifted away and everything settled into place.

"*I'm* sorry," he said. "There was a lot of stuff I didn't get either, and all this time I tried to make you the woman I thought I wanted, when all along I loved the woman you are."

She pulled away and grabbed his chin. "Then why didn't you call me?" she shot at him.

"Why didn't you call me?" he countered, the grin never leaving his face.

"You left without even telling me anything. I thought you'd listened to me and given up on us."

"I couldn't support what you were doing with Donavan, no matter how hard I tried, and I didn't see a way past that." He tightened his grip on her again, pulling her back toward him. Man, he was going to spend this entire reception dancing with her. Who cared what her mom thought? Mrs. Pope could run a wedding or two on her own.

She tilted her head back. "Did you say you loved me?" she asked in a whisper.

He nodded.

She took a shuddering breath and slowly let it out. "When you make a declaration like that, you're supposed to do it right. Say my last name and everything. At least that's how it is in every romance novel I've ever read."

He chuckled. "You? Read romance novels?"

"Where do you think all my great wedding ideas come from?" That mischievous smile reeled him in every time. "I love you, Sophie Pope."

She closed her eyes and sighed. "Mmmm. Me too."

He rested his forehead against hers. "'Me too'? That's all you're going to say?" he said against her lips.

"I love you, David Savage." She reached her arms around his neck.

He didn't wait a second longer to kiss her. Even while his best friend whistled from behind him. When he'd kissed her enough to make up for not saying goodbye and for their hello, and then a bit more, he led her to the dance floor and stayed there with her until the band stopped playing.

chapter twenty-one

THREE MONTHS *Later*

Sophie stood on her tiptoes and glared down the long hallway. She leaned forward when the locker room door opened, but the player who exited wasn't David. She frowned and rocked back again.

"Anxious or something?" Ty asked from beside her. Sophie had met her and Anthony in L.A. to watch David's major league debut for the Atlanta Braves.

"Seriously, though," Sophie scowled. "How long does it take for a guy to shower and get dressed? You'd think he didn't miss me at all."

"You're so dramatic, Sophie. You saw him before the game," Anthony teased.

"For like ten minutes. Not enough after not seeing him for over a month. Next time *I* book the plane tickets."

Ty chuckled and slid an arm around Sophie's shoulder. "Get used to it."

Sophie slumped forward and laughed at herself. "He's taking so long."

"Cut the guy some slack," Anthony said from behind them. "He did pretty good for his first night in the Majors. I think. I fell asleep for a lot of the game."

"He was pretty awesome," Sophie agreed. The door opened again, but neither of the two guys who came out were her boyfriend. She chewed on her bottom lip. She hadn't seen him in weeks, and if the Braves made it into the post-season, she had a lot more weeks of loneliness left before he came home for the off-season.

"How's work?" Ty asked, and Sophie guessed she did it to pass the time for them.

"Great. Did David tell you guys that Mom gave me my own office? Well, kind of. I have to share it with her assistant, Jessica." Sophie cast a grateful look at Ty. "Mom's going to put me in charge of some advertising we're going to do over the next few months."

"Sounds like she's keeping you busy. Do you even have time to miss David?" Ty asked.

"Of course. I've decided we should've never let him choose baseball. The football season is shorter, right?" Sophie pulled a mock pout while the other two laughed. Despite the diversion of the brief conversation, Sophie's gaze snapped back to the locker room door when it opened again. This time David did exit, his moppy hair still wet from his shower and his bag slung over his shoulder.

Sophie didn't waste any time. Her heels clicked furiously over the linoleum floor as she hurried down the hall. He met her in a few long strides, lifting her up and holding her tight.

"It is so good to see you," he said, setting her down and then pulling her face up to meet his in a kiss. "I missed you."

She stared at him, savoring these few moments she would have him to herself before they went out with Anthony and Ty for dinner. She tried not to think about how she'd have only a few hours with him before he had to get on a plane to Seattle. "You did great," she said. "I was hoping you'd totally bomb everything so they'd kick you off the team and you could come home."

"Don't tell me you're cheering against us making it all the way to the World Series." He pretended to be shocked.

"Never," she promised, kissing him again. And then again. It took several more seconds to come back to the topic at hand. "If you make it to the World Series, I'm coming to every game."

"Seems like a bit of a commitment, flying across the country to watch me play baseball." David's brown eyes softened along with his voice.

"Well, yeah," she said with a sigh. "But you might be worth it."

He smiled against her lips as he moved in for another kiss. "Good to hear."

As he pulled her even closer, Sophie melted into him with one thought.

Totally worth it.

acknowledgments

A big thanks to my cousin David, who's such a cool guy that I couldn't help it when some of his personality spilled into his character namesake—and so in turn caused lovely readers to beg for his story. And Megan, please don't be jealous of Sophie. She's just pretend.

Again, thank you to my friends and family willing to loan their names to the voices in my head: David Allred, DJ Savage, Sean Savage, Nikki Sanford, Savanna Rose Savage, Debbie Allred, and Shayli McArthur.

Thank you so much to my writing support network, specifically my CPs, Kaylee Baldwin and Gina Denny, who are the best at it. To Donna Weaver, who read this so long ago she probably doesn't even remember. To Krista Jensen, who jumped on board last minute to give me an extra set of eyes that I desperately needed and some very sound advice. To the ladies who have been there and done that, who are always willing to give me advice, soothe my ruffled feathers, and talk me down from ledges: Sarah Eden, Jenny Moore, Melanie Jacobson, and Krista Jensen. They're superstars, for real. To my accountability partner and partner in crime, Tiffany Odekirk, who keeps me on task and also off task.

The hugest thank you and group hug to the people at Covenant. My superhero editor Stacey Owen, PR expert Stephanie Lacey, the amazingly talented cover lady, Christina Marcano, and those many people who work behind the scenes to make my books so great. I can't express my gratitude enough.

Thank you, thank you to my family who supports me with all their hearts. My parents, Doug and Robyn Savage, my siblings, and their spouses. My brother DJ, who continues to add his knowledge and expertise to keep things on the up and up. Of course, there's my better half, Adam, who never doubts me and bends over backwards so I can make my dreams come true. To my boys—A.J., Jaxen, and Tre—who flatter me beyond words by loving writing too.

And always, my gratitude to my Heavenly Father, who blessed me with a talent and led me to the way to use it.

more by raneé s. clark

about the author

In a house overrun by boys, it shouldn't come as a surprise that Raneé loves football and enjoys watching (and playing!) other sports as well, like basketball and baseball. When she's not chauffeuring three busy boys to various activities (and sometimes while she is!), Raneé is either writing, reading (usually romance), obsessing over clothes in the form of her online boutique, or figuring out how to get a Crumbl cookie in rural Wyoming. When her real-life love interest can drag her away from imaginary worlds, she doesn't mind spending some time with him in the great outdoors that he loves.